The
CRESCENT
MOON

Realm of the Prophets
Book I

E J Doble

Also by E J Doble:

THE BLOOD AND STEEL SAGA
1: *The Fangs of War*
2: *The Horns of Grief*

REALM OF THE PROPHETS
1: *The Crescent Moon*

Cover design and illustration by: Liam Fraser @lafgraphic

For Bonnie,

Thank you for fifteen years of showing me purpose
— I miss you every day.

The City of Arbash, desert kingdom of the Prophets, lay on the western-most tip of the greatest desert the world had ever known. If one stood on the parapets of the eastern walls, looking out to the distant horizon, they would find nothing but sand and cloudless blue skies. If one looked on a map of the Known World, detailed by the hands of scribes nearly a millennia ago, they would find Arbash as a lone red dot aside a striking blue sea, consumed by the great nothingness of the desert beyond. A single city, lined with groves of olives, clementines and grapes, fed by an underground spring that had kept the grass green for hundreds of years. The winding, terraced earth unravelling down the hill like an old carpet, until finally spilling out under an old sea-arch into a shingle cove of painted rocks. And, from there, out onto the endless waves, an aquamarine sea the colour of stardust.

The most beautiful sight of the Known World.

It was said, in the old stories, that it was that archway out to the sea that convinced the old Prophets to settle there. That the great migrators of a forgotten era looked upon that portal into the heavenly realm, and saw in there a reflection of their own soul, so pure and bright. That as they stepped onto that parched ground, a tiny spring pulled up from the earth and bathed the plateaus in reams of fresh water. That as they set their camps under the stars, fields of clovers and crocus flushed the land in dazzling streaks of purple. And, when they awoke that morning and set the first stone down that would eventually found an entire kingdom, it seemed to fuse in place as if it had always belonged there.

And the City of Arbash, was born.

From a single, shield-sized stone, the city bloomed formidably, like the clover fields that bathed the landscape around it. Towers pierced the sky, capped in rivets of bronze; a length of wall appeared as thick as it was tall, interspersed with gatehouses and parapets as far as the eye dared look; squat two-storey houses and burgeoning citadels emerged along gold-lined streets of stone, opening out into wide squares and gardens of lush green pomegranate trees. It was a city that seemed to rise from the dry earth like a lotus flower, drawing its way up to the surface and blossoming out in its radiance for all the world to see. A place of peace and wonder; a place of awe and grandiosity. It was, upon its completion, a city like the desert had never known. Built by the tireless hands of the Prophets.

Their greatest masterpiece.

And when it was done, so the stories go, these wanderers lay their tools down on the hillside and meditated for many nights out on the fields where the clovers grew. They sat under the stars, watching the moon blanket the sea in brushstrokes of silver.

And as they sat, passing deep within the alcoves of their souls, a tiny sapling knotted its way through the earth behind them. It reached up with prying hands, weaving and intertwining, sprouting tiny leaves with tiny green buds in the blinding sun. And the Prophets, unaware of the tree, continued to explore the realms of their minds — even as the branches passed overhead and cast them all in shadow. They found peace and time and space; answers to questions that had never been asked; the elucidation of a soul transcending the bounds of mortal life. The tree, in turn, thread its roots between their legs, branches folding down as if to touch them, pulling skyward to catch the sun. A beauty, as one became bound to the other, and the city walls and the shimmering sea bowed their heads to the wanderers who had come to solve the riddles of the infinite. Time seemed to elapse without direction.

Until one day, they were gone.

The story never explained why, or how, the Prophets disappeared from beneath the shade of that great tree. Some believed they ascended to the stars one night, and unlocked the truth of the world; others believed they walked down to the cove at the base of the hill, and simply swept out to sea. A few believed they were absorbed within the boughs of the tree itself: that in their place, the tree would live on as the eternal sentinel, looking out over the city they had built for generations to come.

The greatest kingdom the desert had ever seen.

And as centuries passed, and the new wanderers of the dunes stumbled upon that forgotten sanctuary on their lowly quest to survive, all that came before them was forgotten. As they entered the homes and manned the walls and traded in the squares of that vast city, they never once asked whose hand had built it. When they went out into the fields and ploughed the soft earth and sowed their seeds, they never once asked who had raised the spring that brought so much life there in the first place. When the shadows of disease swept through the streets and they closed the heavy iron gates, they never once asked who had left the gates open so they could settle there in the beginning.

From the edge of the plateau, the old sentinel tree watched it all unravel: watched as humanity revealed itself, settling in the great city of the Prophets long-forgotten. Watching their revelations and beliefs; their order and their chaos; the unfathomable wealth and the glaring depravity. Looking on, with the eternal souls of the first wanderers nestled within its boughs, as the sanctuary where it had been born transformed in a few short lifetimes.

Yet still the tree remained there, steadfast and pensive, awaiting something more. That this, the great euphoria of human existence, was but a grain of sand in time. Something was coming, and the souls within its boughs could sense it. A time of beauty, and of terror. A time of great turmoil and change. A time when it would all reach an end.

And a new Prophet, would come.

I

THE HERMIT

I

The sun glistened overhead, like the hopeful eyes of a new mother first seeing her child, as another day passed in the city of Arbash – the greatest kingdom the world had ever known. Its weaving rays fell across the walled courtyard far below, dancing across carved sandstone and patterned walkways. Bushels of juniper flickered like jade flames along the outskirts. Squares of vibrant green grass swayed soundlessly with tiny yellow flowers pushing up through their ranks. And at the centre, splaying outwards with thick branches and perfectly oval leaves, the prideful shape of a hibiscus tree gazed out over the courtyard, its pink-orange flowers gaping like tiny whales to capture the virulence of the sun.

Tucked away beneath its bushelled little branches, a young girl sat in the shade whispering quietly to herself, watching the tiny flutters of hummingbirds dance through the under croft around her. They were tiny specks of light dicing through the air, like glittering gold coins in a merchant's pocket. Moving so quickly, their tiny beaks diving into the hibiscus flowers for the nectar pooled in its heart. A blink, and they were there feeding; another, and they were gone again, zipping off into the sun with the shimmer of riches across their backs. And in that time, they spent little more than a heartbeat studying the small girl who sat beneath the boughs of their tree. The little girl watching them whimsically.

Her favourite place to be.

Listening out to their sweet chirps, the girl turned suddenly to attention, alerted to the sound of footsteps and the call of her name.

"My'ala!"

Her mother's voice, soft as silk, calling out from the doorway of the house.

"Where are you, my dear!"

"I'm here, Mumma!" the young girl called back, whispering an apology to the startled birds as she crawled from under the hibiscus tree and emerged out into the light.

"There you are! Whatever were you doing under there?" her mother asked, beaming a smile as bright as the moon.

"Watching the birds, Mumma… the little ones with the fast wings that feed on the flowers."

"Ah, the hummingbirds, such beautiful creatures! So full of spirit… much like you in fact, my dear." She closed her eyes, beckoning her over with a wave of the hand. "But it's time to come inside now: your father is due home shortly, and I'm sure you want to see him."

"Yes I do! I want to ask you both something!"

"Is that so?" A quizzical grin. "Well, best come inside and see him then."

My'ala showed a row of shining white teeth, and followed the winding stone path through the grass toward the back door with dainty steps. She stopped just before her mother, who bent low to the ground and bundled her up in her arms, squeezing tightly.

"You're so wonderful, Mi-Mi, so full of love," her mother cooed pleasantly, unwrapping her embrace. "But even then, you really must learn to keep your clothes clean…"

With deeply-tanned hands and silver bangles, she brushed against My'ala's dress in long strokes, trying to clear the sandy dust that coated the cloth like flour.

The young girl stepped back, shying away. "I can do it myself, Mumma, you know," she said firmly, fluttering her dress with her hands to release the dust. "See? All gone."

Her mother stood, nodding slowly. "You're right, my dear, you can do it yourself… I guess I just forget how grown-up you are."

"I'm nearly ten!"

"Yes, I know! And I wonder where the years have gone."

"You don't look that old, Mumma."

"And what does that mean, young lady?"

My'ala blushed, cheeks the colour of roses – her mother laughed aloud.

"I only joke of course, my dear." She tugged at her cheek.

"How could I ever stay mad at you…"

As the words fell from her lips, the sound of an unhooked latch echoed out from deeper within the house, and a familiar voice called out from the hallway. The young girl looked to her mother with a contagious warmth in her eye and, without a word spoken, slipped her shoes off and dashed through the house toward the front door. As she turned from the spacious living room out into the corridor beyond, she squeaked at the sight of her father placing his bags down and bolted toward him at full speed, so that he only just managed to bring his arms round to catch her in time.

"Oh, hello my little Mi-Mi!" he rumbled, pulling her up onto his chest so the wisps of his beard tickled her forehead. "What a lovely introduction."

"Hi Dadda," she replied, face buried in his collar, clinging to him like a cub. "How was your day?"

"Very polite of you to ask: my day went well, thank you. Business as usual." He lowered the girl down gently to the floor, following her expectant eyes.

"Did you sell many tools?"

"I did indeed, Mi-Mi. Even sold some of those new machines today, too. Remember the ones I told you about?"

"The ones you have to pull along with a big rope? That spin the soil over in big loops?"

"Those ones exactly, yes. I sold three of those today."

"There'll be a fleet of your father's products out there one day, my dear," her mother said, gliding past her and landing a kiss on her father's lips. "Just you wait and see."

"I think you do me a great overestimation there," the

father said humbly, batting the comment aside.

"Far from it: you're ahead of your competitors by several dozen. Soon they'll be coming to *you* looking for the next great way to sow seeds."

"It's not a dying trade, that's for sure… always more mouths to feed in a place like Arbash." He smiled, looking down to his daughter. "Speaking of, I think that's about time for dinner…"

"Yes please!" My'ala beamed.

"Any preference?"

"Something light please," the mother informed, holding her stomach. "The system is quite upset today."

"Can we have gojan fruit? It's my favourite," the young girl added. "You make the best risotto with it."

"Gojan fruit is definitely not *light*, Mi-Mi, and I don't think your mother wants anymore upset than she's already having," her father replied. My'ala looked to the floor, conceding. "That being said, I'm sure it'll find its way onto your plate very soon. Now go rally your brother and sister for me, would you?"

"Yes, Dadda."

My'ala turned from him and, with a skittering of small feet, launched herself down the hallway and up the narrow flight of stairs to the second floor. She bounded like a mountain goat, throwing off the muttered concerns of her mother below and sprung up the last few steps in great strides.

Moving left in a half-turn, she came to a grass-woven door with the black insignia of a dolphin painted across its outward face. She had never understood the significance of it, or bothered to ask, but something about it puzzled her nonetheless.

I've never seen a dolphin, she considered. *Maybe my sister has.* A sharp intake of breath.

If I ask her, maybe she'll show me too…

She knocked twice, and with a delicate hand she prized the door open and peered inside. The room was very tidy, with a stack of paper in one corner and several carved drawers in the other, the back wall next to her occupied by a low bed with purple woven sheets. Through the open window, a light breeze trickled in and spun the stained-glass ornaments hanging there, depicting animals and stars and phases of the moon. My'ala had wanted some of her own for a very long time, wanting to know how to make them for herself – and, as her eyes crossed the room to the desk at the far wall, she saw that someone else knew that too.

"You always look at those when you come in here," her sister said with a smile. "We'll have to get you your own for your room sometime soon."

"I want to know how to make them, too, Su'la," the girl replied, "so I can have as many as I want whenever I want."

"Then I'll teach you how to – it's quite easy, you know."

"I'll make millions of them."

"Is that right?" A smirk. "What will you make them of?"

"I…" She stopped for a moment, pondering the question, until the answer came to her as obvious as anything. "I would make hummingbirds, and hibiscus flowers, and juniper. I would make lots of them."

"A very fitting selection to make in stained glass, My'ala… good choice," Su'la said appreciatively, nodding her head. "Now, was there something you wanted?"

"Yea, dad's home, dinner will be ready soon."

"Perfect, I'll be down in a few minutes."

"Okay."

My'ala closed the door again, turning and bounding off toward the next room on the opposite side of the stairs. Another grass-woven door greeted her there, this time depicting the squawking head of a crow. She grimaced.

Who would want a crow? Crows are loud and annoying, and like to caw at people who get too close. A smirk.

Like my brother.

She knocked twice and pushed the door ajar, and the distinct sigh of irritation prickled in her ears. The room beyond was darker, littered with stray clothes, a red-woven quilt left untucked on the bed. In the far corner, hanging aloft like a strange ghost, the handmade shadow of a suit of armour stood studying her intently, several of its pieces still unfinished. The sight made her flinch, as if it were a real person with real and evil eyes.

"What is it?" her brother's voice echoed. Looking a few feet to the right, she found him squat against the wall reading fervently from a small book.

"I just came to tell you dad is home, and dinner will be ready soon," My'ala muttered in reply, then frowned. "What book is that, Dur'al?"

"Do you *really* want to know?"

"Yes."

"*The Marshal, His Excellency's Field Guide to Being the Best Recruit.*"

Her frown deepened. "Is that for the army?"

"Yea, it is. Very important stuff about being the best. It would go *over* your head."

"I thought you were told not to look at that stuff anymore – that the army was a dangerous place."

He sighed. "The world is a dangerous place, Mi, and it always has been. We never know what comes next, or what waits just around the corner. For me, I'd want to join up so I could do my bit to make it less dangerous for people. I'd take action, rather than cower from it like..." He caught himself, holding his tongue – waving the unspoken words away like a bad smell. "Never mind. Just... tell dad I'll be down in a few minutes, please."

"Okay, I will."

She closed the door again, stopping at the top of the stairs for a moment.

Cowering? Who's cowering from what? she thought. *What does Dur'al know that I don't?*

She descended the staircase, reciting the questions over and over in her head – the answers to which she would not know for five long years.

They reconvened at the table a short while later, flocking to the table like pigeons to feast on the day's best pickings. Their father had prepared an assortment of foods for them to pick and choose at their behest: a flat spice-bread that sizzled when it tore; grapes of a number of colours, some of which had been fermented in sour-stones to draw out their sweetness; vo'zan bird meat, stewed in a sticky nectar and grilled with peppers; a spread of green leaves and herbed vines that remained — much to their mother's disapproval — largely untouched.

They all settled for dinner in the alcove overlooking the back garden, picking at food as they went discussing the day's affairs. For the most part, it was Su'la and their father talking about larger-than-life politics that My'ala found both eclipsing and completely odious. So she instead took much greater comfort in positioning herself perfectly to watch the hummingbirds weave through the hibiscus tree outside, grape juices dripping down her chin in little streams.

I wonder if they have family meals and chirp about their days, she thought, giggling at the sizzle of the spice-bread as she swallowed a mouthful down. *Little bird meetings about how nice the flowers are today.*

"You ought to look like a hummingbird with how much time you spend watching them," her mother said at her side, running a hand down her back. "Although I must admit, they are rather captivating... like tiny gold stars."

"Dad used to say they were like gold coins from a merchant's pocket," she replied. "There one minute and gone the next."

"That's because your father is an awful cynic when he wants to be, and thinks everyone's a crook..."

"What's that?" her father called from the other end of the table. "My ears are burning."

"Hummingbirds, Dadda, like coins," My'ala responded, still fixated on them dancing through the tree. "That's what you used to tell me."

"It is..." He took a mouthful of vo'zan meat, the nectar

pooling at the corners of his mouth. "And the great thing about them, is that although possessing the same allure as money does, they have none of the greediness that goes with it."

"I've been reading something about that," Su'la informed, gesturing with herb-coated fingers. "Theories about how money affects the mind… apparently it has similar effects to drinking *pos'thum* and being lurid… the brain goes into a trance, almost. It's quite interesting."

"Oh, yes, marvel at she, the fountain of knowledge," Dur'al interjected, rolling his eyes. "Labouring over books for the sake of a few pretty facts…"

Su'la scowled. "Just because I'm reading something *useful,* Dur'al… rather than you, burying your head in those army field guides all day."

Their father produced an expression not too dissimilar to indigestion, eyes tracing over to his son. "I thought you promised us that you'd be getting rid of those books."

"Yes, father, and I have got rid of them for the most part," he challenged. "But I don't see the need in getting rid of *all* of them. It's still something I enjoy reading and learning about, even if you have banished the idea from the house that I may ever consider joining up…"

"And that is how it shall remain." His tone was definitive, commanding – My'ala shied away, sensing confrontation. "I won't have my son, or any member of my family, wasting their life like that."

"I'm fourteen, father… surely that should count?"

"And your older sister is sixteen, and I expect the same of her." A pause – their father sighed. "In the eyes of the law, once you are eighteen rain's gone you are considered an *adult,* and at that point you may do whatever you like with your life. But here, now, as a child under my roof, I will not entertain any notion of you joining up."

"It's not really fair, though, is it?"

"It's not about what *you* think is fair—"

"*Anyway,*" their mother interrupted, ending the conversation in a single strike. "Now that that discussion is *sorted...* I believe, My'ala, you had something you wanted to ask us."

Drawn from the hummingbirds by the call of her name, the young girl turned to the attentive gazes of her family and seemed to shrink in her seat. She flitted between them awkwardly, rubbing her feet together to calm her nerves. It was only with her mother's steady hand clasping her own under the table, that she found the courage to speak.

"I was wondering, as it's nearly my tenth rain," My'ala said slowly, "if I would be allowed to go out... into the fields... by myself. I know it was Su'la's eleventh rain when she was allowed to, and Dur'al had to wait until he was ten, and... but I've been wanting to do this for a really long time and, and I just wanted to ask and see..."

A silence descended for a moment. The two other children looked between their parents with quizzical eyes, trying to pick apart their reaction. Su'la offered a quick smile to her little sister to keep her calm; Dur'al did nothing, and waited to see how it would unfold instead.

Her father, looking up to the warm auburn glow of his partner's eyes, produced a flicker of a smile and shrugged slowly. "Going out beyond the city walls on your own is a big step, Mi-Mi... are you sure you'd be ready to do that?"

My'ala nodded cautiously, looking to her mother.

"It was only this morning I looked at you and said how fast you were growing up," the woman replied, running a hand through her deep brown hair. "You are a force unto yourself, my dear." She looked up to their father and shrugged in return. "A turn of the sun, shall we say?"

"I think that's reasonable, for the fledgling's first flight from the nest," he replied. "What say you two?"

"She's ready," Su'la replied with a wink.

"Sure," Dur'al said noncommittally.

"Then I believe we have an agreement..."

My'ala's eyes shone with glee.

"You are allowed one turn of the sun outside the walls, Mi-Mi, and not a moment more. Stay within sight of the city gates at all times, and make sure to bring your little slip out with you, so people know who you are and a guard can help you get home if you're lost. Have you got it?"

Pulling through the folding pocket of her sage-coloured dress, she plucked the identification card out and displayed it proudly for all to see, grin plastered to her face like honey.

"Then if that's the case... I guess you're free to go."

My'ala leapt from her seat and embraced her mother with a huge squish of the arms, before skirting round the long table to do likewise to her father.

Stepping away, she skipped through to the next room and waved them all goodbye, the elation so full in her heart she felt almost fit to explode. Sticking the card back in her wide pocket, she passed into the hallway and opened the front door.

And with a few more steps, she was off.

II

The southern gate opened out onto the edge of a plateau, falling away like a deck of cards toward the fruit trees cascading down the valley. Even from a distance, one could see the sublime orange rounds of the clementine trees, and the dashed spots of grapes coiled along vine-like branches. Other plants had begun to cultivate, too, in the upper reaches where water was sparser: a strange shrub sprouting grey-brown fruits not too dissimilar to moth cocoons, and sad looking clusters of shrivelled fruits baking on the splayed branches of trees. They were the new crops, the seeds of which blew across on desert sands to nestle in the semi-soft soil at the sanctuary's edge. Many had come and gone before, growing sporadically and failing to make any foothold before they withered away. It was a known cycle to the people of Arbash. Yet some, like the moth cocoons, had found a way to survive.

And My'ala, in an exhilarant daze at the prospect of being outside the city walls, didn't even notice the new crops spotting the outline of the desert to the east. She hardly took in the orange rounds and dappled spots of fruit weaving across the valley before her, or the high cliffs that banked either side from which vultures the size of camels ejected and coursed over the winds lazily above.

Instead, the young girl turned back to face the gateway that she just passed through, the identification slip still flapping loosely in her hand, and took in the enormity of it all. The City of Arbash — a city she had known from storybooks, and had traversed the inner streets of a hundred times' over – forming in front of her, impossibly large at every angle. A winding wall like nothing she had seen, stretching out to either side like God-King the Creator's adoring embrace. Towers and spires rising up higher than the sun itself; rippling waves of heat rising from every rooftop and bronze-plated point she could find. It was a terrific, terrifying sight.

A place she had never known, yet every day called home.

I never saw it like this, when I came out here with Dadda last year, she thought, almost falling backwards. *I didn't think anything in the world could be built this big.*

I wonder who did build it?

But the thought came and went almost as quickly as the Prophets themselves, as My'ala turned slowly to the west and gasped at the sight she beheld.

A sea of purest blue, bluer than any dye she had ever known, spilling out to a horizon of gold and silver light. A cove of painted pebbles: soft pastel pinks and speckled greys arranged almost methodically across the shoreline. And a sea-arch, taller than even the highest point of the city at her side, bridging the cliffs to create a perfect circle at the base of the valley below.

How have I not noticed it before? she thought whimsically, eyes like gaping moons. *I thought it was only in the stories… I didn't realise it was real.* A daring thought rose in her chest that she exhaled through with a smile. *I'll go there soon. I'll ask Mumma to take me down to the rocks and see the sea. I'll put my hands in it and feel how blue it is. I'll imagine I'm a ship going to the horizon, and watch it go on forever and ever.*

Someday.

She nodded, forcing herself to look away – longing to run down there and be consumed by the beauty of the water, but knowing to do so would be untruthful to her parents, and paint her as a reckless child flying too close to the sun. *I cannot ruin this opportunity,* she thought, controlling her feelings. *If I do a bad thing, I might not be allowed back out here. I can't risk that. I must be patient.*

All good things shall come.

My'ala turned to the south, back to the terraced fields of clementine and grapes, and walked towards the first row of bushes snaking off down the path. She let her hand fall loose, pulling through the branches and the tiny, droplet-shaped leaves. It tickled across her fingertips, pulling at vines and tracing the balls of oranges.

Caught on something for a moment: the young girl pulled it free to reveal the tiny red shard of a grape, that she pushed through her lips and pressed against her tongue pleasantly. It was sharp at first, souring on her tongue with a wince. But slowly, collectively, its sweeter notes came through, and she brimmed with joy at the taste.

Just ahead, the crops seemed to climb higher suddenly, snaking outwards in wide ranks. Looking back to the city behind, My'ala hardly realised as she stumbled absently up the small hill, parting ways with the row of fruits.

In a daze, she floated elegantly forward, turning again to the valley ahead of her, the steady rise just ahead...

And the ancient tree sat at its very top, white as porcelain clouds.

My'ala frowned. *A tree? All the way out here?* She walked purposefully up to it, studying the overhanging branches pointing out toward the sea, and the gnarled roots that bent out over the dry earth like snake coils. With its bark parched and worn, and its tiny green-black leaves silhouetted in the sun, My'ala looked up to it with glowing eyes and marvelled at its form. *It's so old… I wonder if it's older than my parents. Maybe even older than the city. Maybe…*

But how?

"It's quite something, isn't it?"

The young girl shuddered, eyes snapping from the ancient tree to the base of its trunk.

Where an old man sat, older than any man she had ever seen, concealed in a faded-red robe with white trims like fishing lines. She saw little of his face, beyond the swarm of straggled grey hair forming his beard the ends of which tickled at his feet. Fixed to the spot, she wondered for a moment if he was just a figment of her imagination. He did not move nor acknowledge the young girl beyond the words he had spoken, but My'ala was certain she saw the tiny twist of a smile at his cheeks. How she had not noticed him before, she was not sure.

Perhaps he fell from the tree, or pulled up from its roots, she thought, brushing her dress down.

Perhaps he is magic.

"Who are you?" My'ala inquired, squaring her eyes.

The man did not respond for some time. "I am a traveller," he replied, voice soft and echoing like her mother's. "My name is Artemis, young one… Artemis the Hermit. It's a pleasure to meet you."

The name seemed important. "What's a *hermit?*"

"A hermit is someone who does not wish to be in any one

place for any length of time, so chooses instead to wander the lands and sleep under the stars, listening to the rhythms of nature like music."

A wanderer? "So, you have no home?"

"I do, my dear. The desert is my home… it is just not the home you're referring to." A smirk. "I do not have a house, if that's what you mean."

"Then you do not have a family?"

Something like remembrance crossed his gaze. "I did once, a very long time ago… but have not for many years now. I seek no counsel in love, for that is a fool's errand. No: I have love for night skies and desert oases and sand-surfing beasts the likes of which you city-folk have never known. And I do so, by all accounts, *alone.*"

"That sounds… lonely."

"Perhaps it can be, at times."

"So, why do it?"

He pursed his lips. "Because it's rather remarkable, the things you can learn from this world, when you live and breathe its very soul every day…"

She frowned, not understanding what the man called Artemis meant. How he seemed to talk in rhymes that made her head spin; how he spoke of the desert and the sands like it were really his home. *Perhaps he is confused, or lost… or perhaps he doesn't know how to form his words.*

How strange.

"Why do you sit under this tree?" My'ala inquired again.

"You ask a lot of questions, girl."

"That's because I wish to know about the desert and the world you speak of. I want to learn. It's my first time out here, you know."

"Then you are very brave to do so, miss…?"

"My'ala. That is my name."

"Ah, My'ala… *'kissing stars'*… I have not heard a name like that in a long time."

The girl scrunched her brow. "What are you talking about?"

An accepting expression. "I see you are quite confused, my dear… and I can understand why. I doubt you've come across someone like me before," the man called Artemis acknowledged. "So if you will, or feel happy to, then please take a seat alongside me, and I shall happily answer any questions you have. I'm sure you have some reluctance to do so, as your parents will have rightly told you not to engage with strangers… but the choice is entirely yours."

The Hermit turned to her then, revealing his full face beyond the loose strands of grey, and My'ala gasped. Not for his wrinkled forehead or blemished cheeks, nor for the large scar across the bridge of his nose – she gasped, instead, because of his eyes. They were completely black, laced with swirls of deep blue like a night-glazed sea, the tiny twinkles of stars shimmering within their rapture. Even in the all-encompassing light of the mid-afternoon sun, they were incredibly dark and foreboding. The young girl sensed herself almost falling into them and drifting off into the night sky. *How magical,* she thought.

A man with the stars in his eyes.

Cautiously, wondering what had possessed her, My'ala lowered herself to the dusty earth and sat cross-legged where she was, a few feet from the old man. She studied him intently, locked to his patient eyes, the taste of bitter grape still sat in her gums.

"Why are you here?" she said slowly, too afraid to ask about the man's starry eyes.

"I am here, because of this…" the Hermit replied, turning and laying a gnarled hand against the tree. "Because this is no ordinary tree, you see. Not even remotely…"

"What tree is it?"

"It's called a Sentinel Tree, and it's the only one of its kind to ever exist. A very special plant indeed."

My'ala peered up into its boughs, the bark spilling over like marble, and squinted. "How does it live out here? Mumma said there hasn't been enough water here to ever grow big trees. Only fruit trees."

"And your mother would be correct: no tree could survive out here living off of water alone, beyond the small bushes you see in the fields before you. And that's one of the many reasons why this tree here is so magical: because it doesn't require water to survive at all."

"How does it exist, then? I thought all plants need water."

"All plants need *fuel*, my dear." The old man wagged a finger. "That's the difference."

"Then what… *fuel*… does this tree need?"

The Hermit made to explain to her, but stopped suddenly, his lips sealing shut. Closing his eyes, he raised a hand instead, offering his own question. "What do you know of how the city was first built, My'ala?"

"I don't know anything about it." She paused. "What has that got to do with the tree?"

A polite smile. "Well, it's a long story, and not one you

need to know every detail about, but what you do need to know is that the city behind you was first built by five wanderers of the desert – and these people were called the Prophets."

"The *Prophets…*" She rolled the name over her tongue, pondering. "You travel the desert: are you a Prophet?"

A muted laugh. "Oh, no, no, I am nothing like those people. No, the Prophets were far more important than any commoner like me. They built the city with their bare hands and raised the water from the earth to feed the soil. Their knowledge is far beyond me."

"They sound… powerful."

"They were, yes, incredibly so… but they were also very human. Thoughtful, reflective, intuitive. Very much like us, in a way. And the reason why I tell you this story, and explain this to you, is because those same Prophets, when they had finished building the city, came to this spot where we are now sat and began to meditate. Do you know about meditation?"

"My sister does that. She sits on the floor and closes her eyes and counts goats."

It was the Hermit's turn to frown. "Counts goats?"

"Yea. That's what I do when *I* go to sleep."

"*Ah*, I see." A broader smile. "Meditation and sleep are very different things, my dear. Sleep is rest, to unravel your mind and your body for the next day. Meditation on the other hand is taking the space to look into yourself, and your thoughts, and make sense of the world around you. To ask questions, mainly, hoping to find answers."

"Oh, that is different," My'ala considered. "So when my

sister meditates, she asks questions?"

"Most likely, yes."

"But who answers her?"

"She does."

Her brow furrowed. "She answers *herself?*"

"That's why people meditate. To ask questions of themselves, and find their own answers. Your sister does it, I do it… you may do it as well, someday, when you have your own questions."

"But I *ask* my questions, because I'm only young. I don't know the answers."

The Hermit nodded, meeting her eyes. "But there are some questions, My'ala, that don't *have* answers."

My'ala thought on the man's words for some time, feeling the warm blaze of the sun across her cheek. "Is that what the Prophets were looking for?" she inquired, pushing her thumbs against her ankles.

"Yes it was: they sat under this tree, and asked the questions that no-one has answers to. What binds the world; what connects life; what drives progress."

"Big questions, then."

"The biggest questions we can ask, yes. And amongst those ponderings, they also asked the one question I am now here to try and find the answer to…"

"What's that?"

A coy smile. "The meaning of *life.*"

My'ala felt the cogs turn in her mind, instinctively seeking an answer despite the Hermit's words.

"There is no meaning, though," she declared eventually. "We are born from the matter of our parents, and that matter returns to the world when we die. We are just essence, my Mumma says. Our purpose is just… to *be*."

"A good insight, and very thoughtful… but is that truly all that there is? If the meaning of life is just *to be,* then your life is no more complex than a blade of grass, or an olive bush. You will live, exist, sustain… but what else? Our mortal souls are very different. You must admit, my dear, that we are infinitely more complex and interesting than *grass.*"

"That's obvious… I think."

"I agree. Because we have thought. We have minds, and eyes, and stomachs. Every choice we make has a meaning." The Hermit paused. "For example, why did you decide to come out of the city today? Why did you decide to walk south to this tree, instead of west to the cove? Why did you choose to sit and talk to me of these things?"

My'ala thought hard, a sense of unease rising in her chest. "I… I don't know. I think I was curious. I think I wanted to see what was here. I want to be more grown-up."

"Well, My'ala, I can say without a doubt you are certainly more grown-up than I was expecting when you first climbed that hill. More grown-up than most adults, at that."

She beamed, screwing her nose up.

"But remember that your choice to sit here, with me, and talk about these things… it was a *choice.* Something you did. That gives it purpose, and *meaning.* All of our day-to-day choices have that meaning behind them. But the meaning of life, you see… that's different altogether. Because that's not just one thing. The meaning of life is what guides us, as people, through every *single* choice we make. It's why we're here, and why we do what we do. And *that,* is the one question that I long to find the answer for." He sat back, exhaling softly. "And that is why I sit here, under this great tree, and think."

She shuffled uncomfortably on the spot. "You seek what the Prophets found?"

"I seek all the answers, so I may hope to ascend as they did, and be absorbed into this Sentinel Tree forever."

My'ala gulped. "That's... *scary.*"

"Perhaps, but it's also..." The Hermit looked to her for a moment and stopped, drawing his mouth closed beneath his beard. He watched as the young girl twiddled her thumbs together, looking around anxiously, chewing her bottom lip like a sweet. And a realisation washed over him, like fresh rainwater – and rather than continue his monologue, he chose instead to smile at her.

"But it's also not anything you need to be worrying about," he said simply. "Because you may be grown-up, My'ala, far past your years... but you are still only nine years old, and this is a world as big and scary as it is beautiful."

She nodded, drawing in a quick breath – then, almost accusingly, she frowned. "How do you know I'm nine years old?" she asked.

His smile broadened, acknowledging her perception. The Hermit placed his palm on the tree behind him. "The tree told me so," he replied, "for the tree knows many things. It also knows, for example, that we have been sat here for some time now, and I imagine your mother will be expecting you home soon."

"How does it know?" She leaned forward. "Why does it

tell you these things?"

The Hermit looked up into the boughs and spindly branches of the ancient tree with an almost paternal gaze. "Because, I think, the Prophets like having you here. Because of how you talk, and how you see the world… you ask questions and, despite your inner fears, you want to understand."

She sat staring at him, wide-eyed, then said almost as a whisper: "*they can hear me?*"

"They can… and they think you are rather remarkable, My'ala. And I think they'd quite like to see you again."

"See me again? How?"

"By being here, and coming to this tree. Talking about the world and all of its mysteries." He nodded slowly. "They want to see what you have to say."

"Dadda said that… that if I get back on time then I will be allowed to go out again, and I can come and see you and the tree. We can talk about meaning and things. That would be good." She paused. "Are the Prophets my friends?"

The Hermit tapped his hand against the old trunk. "You know what? I think they just might be." He watched her smile: a joyous, wonderful smile, jostling on the spot. "Now go, back to your parents. Especially if you want to come and see your friends again!"

Almost instinctively, My'ala leapt up onto her feet and brushed the dust from her dress, muttering absent goodbyes as she turned and ran back down the hill. The sun glazed her skin in warm auburn hues, with not a cloud in the sky to mask its glow. And as the grape and clementine bushes fluttered like rolling waves at her side, all the way down to the painted cove at its base, it was almost like running on clouds. She giggled to herself wildly, balancing with open hands. Turning for a moment back to the tree...

And found Artemis the Hermit, was gone.

II

LOVE

Four years later…

Placing her hands on her hips, she studied the sprouting plant in the allotment bed and frowned. It was by far the largest of the crop they had managed to grow that year, with the spindly fronds of its leaves almost reaching her waist. At its base, the sanded earth seemed to bulge upward, hiding the swollen knot of its fruit from sight just below the surface. She had never, in her six years of tending to the allotment with her mother and Su'la, seen a gojan fruit grow to that size.

I don't know what mother's been feeding them, My'ala mused, shaking her head, *but they have definitely made the most of it.*

"C'mon Mi, that's nothing!" her sister teased from a few feet away, tilling the soil further down their family trough.

She wore a red dress with speckled white dots, like a blush rose in the midday heat. "Easy work!"

"Are you joking?" she retorted. "I don't even know if I'm strong enough to get it out. Look at the *size* of it."

"Just use both hands. Give it a few good tugs. You'll be fine!"

Easier said than done, My'ala grimaced.

Such is life, I suppose.

Wrapping her palms around the base of the frond-like leaves, she exhaled slowly through her teeth. She squared her shoulders and buckled her knees. The blaring sun overhead lined her scalp with perspiration, collecting around her eyes like little wells. Why they had decided to harvest in the middle of the day was beyond her, but the desert was often restless and as it turned out, so were they.

Whispering a quiet prayer, she pressed down and jolted upwards suddenly, hoisting the plant with every fibre in her arms.

To find it did not budge an inch.

She lowered herself back into position, regaining her grip on the fronds. Air rasped through her nostrils in frustration. *The thing won't budge.* Tensing her back again, from the base of her skull to her pelvis, she wrenched upwards a second time with gritted teeth.

The gojan fruit shifted slightly, the red-purple skin of its knotted body seeing sunlight for the first time. But still it would not come free.

My'ala wiped her brow, pulling her pale shirt away from her collarbone. The heat was unbearable, a weight across her shoulders. Snapping her hands together again, the young girl hunkered down for round three, with grinding teeth and wild eyes and a vengeful smile across her face. From nearby, her sister watched in quiet amusement as My'ala drew upwards again, roaring with such force that the birds seemed to scatter from the distant rooftops.

And the entire knotted plant burst from the earth like a breach, far easier than expected.

My'ala's heart lurched in her chest. Light shimmered. The massive fruit spun up and over her like a hurling catapult. Her heel, trying to find grip, slipped off the edge of the wooden trough. She found herself in a miniature freefall, eyes spinning across perfect blue skies with nothing but the ground left to greet her...

Until a pair of hands wrapped around her shoulders, and the world seemed to stop.

"Whoa!" a familiar voice cried in her ear. "Go careful, Mi-Mi! You almost squat me."

Her mother eased her onto the tiled floor separating the rows of troughs, squeezing her shoulders. She smiled as reality seemed to return to her daughter's eyes.

"What are you like!" she teased.

"Apologies... Mumma," My'ala replied, steadying her breath, the huge plant like an anchor in her hands. "Can't say I was expecting it to come free so easily."

"No wonder, by the size of it!" Her mother plucked the gojan fruit from the ground and goggled at it, fascinated. It was a strange plant, forming in tight coils like rope, its skin prickly to the touch. The flesh inside was a pearlescent white with purple veins, and it had to be left out in the sun to bake for ten nights before it was even ready to cook. They typically grew to the size of a person's fist.

Not, as is the case here, to the size of a person's head.

"I was wondering about that. What have you been feeding them to make them grow so big?"

"That is a gardener's best kept secret, my dear," she replied with a wink, handing her the fruit. "Bring that one back to the house, and I'll tell you…"

My'ala hefted the gojan fruit onto the countertop with an aching numbness in her arms, and rolled it onto the huge chopping board where her mother waited expectantly with a knife.

"Perfect: all ready to cut and sun," her mother cooed softly, threading strands of her greying hair behind her ear. "I imagine this monster will taste fabulous when it's ready."

"In small doses, ma," Su'la replied from the long stone table nearby, pulling a chair out next to her for her sister to slump into. "Remember your stomach doesn't like too much of that stuff."

"Yes, yes, very true…"

"And when you do go to have some, make sure you have goat-milk around."

"I will, yes…"

"It helps to balance the essence in your stomach."

"I wonder sometimes who the mother is in this house…"

"So, Mumma," My'ala interrupted, slouching into the seat and letting her arms dangle at her side like vines, "I'm intrigued. What is this *'gardener's secret'* you said about?

Because it isn't every day you see a gojan fruit as big as a baby, especially not in allotment soil."

"Certainly so: rare you can grow them at all in such dry conditions."

"Which makes *that* thing quite the anomaly."

A chuckle. "Yes, well, when I first planted and fertilised the thing, I can't say that I was expecting it to grow to *this* size. I mean, it's rather impressive, don't you think?"

"I'd say so. But… how did you do it?"

"Well…" Her mother drew the knife across the fruit's outermost knot, pushing through the skin into the purple-veined flesh beneath. As she did so, it seemed to sizzle like oil, exposed to fresh air for the first time. "Traditionally, gojan fruits grow in ravines where there's a lot of wet soil and heavy sunlight. So, to grow them on the surface, they are given a special type of compost that has to brought from deep underground in the bronze mines. It's nutrient rich stuff, and very expensive to buy… more expensive than we can regularly afford, that's for certain. So it didn't seem to be sustainable. However, as a gardener and botanist, I had a feeling that there must be another, easier way to grow them. So I did a few little… *tests,* shall we say… and I believe – as we can quite clearly see here – that I've found a solution."

"What was it?" Su'la asked, leaning forward in her seat.

Their mother pulled a small wedge from the fruit and rolled it over her palm. "It turns out that gojan fruits are actually best grown in the skin of other gojan fruits, almost like little cocoons. Because it turns out that, although we can't eat it, the skin actually contains a lot of good stuff to help the plant grow again." She smiled, marvelling at the wedge. "And produces incredible specimens like this…"

"That is some admirable work, ma, well done. You know, you could go into the research quarter and present your findings… I imagine they'd be very excited to hear what you've found."

"Yes, well, I suppose," came the non-committal reply, as their mother cut into more sections of the fruit and sighed. "I may do someday, because I know it will probably help some of the farmers with their crops and livelihoods and all that… but for now I just want to marvel at it and take it in. I mean, it's strange to see such closeness and care in the natural world like this. Even though in many ways I suppose, it is the purpose of life for so many plants and creatures across the Known World…"

My'ala's ears tingled, fixating on her mother's words like a bird sensing its nest. *Purpose of life…*

"What did you mean by that?" she asked abruptly.

"By what?"

"The purpose of life… closeness and care. What do you mean by that?"

The greying woman levelled her gaze with her youngest daughter for a moment, a shimmering resplendence in her eye, and something within her seemed to release. My'ala saw her shoulders drop by a fraction; saw the wrinkles around her eyes smooth over like wet sand, a youthfulness returning. Almost like she had longed for someone to ask her that question for her entire life.

And finally, someone has.

"Well, it is what guides all things, is it not?" her mother explained, placing the knife down and turning to full attention. "We are all, as creatures and beings of this land, bound by our essence, by what makes us… and that can only sustain, through *love*."

"And water, and food, and sleep," Su'la said, smirking and wagging her finger. "Don't forget those."

"Ach, ignore your sister, Mi-Mi, she wouldn't know poetry if it kicked her in the head… far too logical is that one." She stuck her tongue out at Su'la, who did the same thing playfully in return. "And you should ignore her, Mi-Mi, because of the one thing your sister misses out. That all things are essentially love's essence."

"What's that supposed to mean?" My'ala inquired.

"Look around you at the life of the desert. A gojan fruit, bound in the skin of another, transforms into an even bigger plant than any before it. Olive bushes link roots like holding hands to transfer nutrients between them where it's needed, so they may all survive. A vo'zan bird is very territorial, only allowing other members of its family in the nest, so that the eggs can be kept at a perfect temperature unique to each group." She smiled. "And when a mother and father have a quiet evening to themselves on a stormy day in the rain, it is love that brings a new life out into the world…"

"Ma, we don't need to know about that!" Su'la exclaimed, waving her hand out to stop her.

"What? It's educational!"

My'ala's cheeks went red. She started laughing, followed by the cackles of her mother, until even her big sister couldn't hide her embarrassment. The young girl sensed her heart grow warm

Mumma has such a way with words.

"But it's true, you see: love and care and family, *they* are what give us purpose and direction in our lives," her mother continued.

"That's not for everyone, though," Su'la scoffed.

"Why isn't it? Your father and brother are the same."

The older daughter frowned. "That's a bit far-fetched. You really think Dur'al believes *love and family* are what makes the sands shift?"

"In his own way, I believe he does – even if he doesn't see it himself." A pause. "Dur'al longs to enlist and join the army, because he wants to make things safer for people. Out of duty, so he says. But what is his duty guided by?"

"The care of others," My'ala finished.

"Exactly! Exactly… and your father, he's the same. We see him as a man who views the world as a deceitful and cruel place. That he sells machines, does business, shakes hands. But why does he do these things, deep down? Not because he believes the newest plough will fix the world, or anything like that." A loving smile. "Because he wants to do his bit to provide for his family: a roof over our heads and food on our table. Because he *cares*, and because, although he's difficult at times, he loves his family more than anything. Just as I do."

"Is that why you serve on the council? To give something back?"

Their mother nodded. "Because I believe, in a position of power, I should do what I can to bring good into this world and care for the people of this city. It gives me such purpose, to know that every day I can help the lives of so many – values, I hope, I have also instilled in you two and your brother." Her eyes passed between them. "In your own, *unique* ways."

"So you genuinely believe everything we do, and who we are… is guided by love and care?" Su'la asked.

"Family is one of the strongest bonds known to us. The care we give, is deeper than even instinct. We would risk everything – our lives, our jobs, our beliefs – to do what we can to love and protect our families and the people we hold close. And why would we do that, something so definitive and personal, if it weren't the most important thing to us?"

"I can't argue with you there." Su'la shrugged. "Although I'll still stick to my own thoughts about it…"

"What does that mean?" My'ala asked.

"It means," came her mother's voice, "your sister doesn't *have* an answer."

"Nor do I believe there is one," she proclaimed. "The simple fact is, we don't know what the meaning or purpose of life is, and I don't think we ever will. There is no definitive answer – because even if there was, it was either lost to the sands of time, or is so *beyond* us that we can never know it anyway. So, I don't bother with an answer at all. We are who we are, and do what we do, for reasons we can never know. And that's it."

My'ala considered their words, jumping between the two sides of the fence like a sprightful goat. *To love and care, and guard those close to you with such focus.* Like a warm fire in a thunderstorm. *To accept your ignorance and deny the possibilities – to act with purpose, but never meaning.* Like a soft pillow with no dreams. *Both credible, but neither complete.*

So which is true?

She found herself lost in the warrens of her mind for a moment, clawing her way back to the surface. The room around her becoming clear again; the sound of voices in her ear.

"…there's nothing wrong with thinking that way. I just don't like giving answers when we don't know what's really true."

Her mother's sigh, so proud and endearing. "As I said, best ignore your sister, Mi-Mi," the greying woman said quietly. "She doesn't understand the *poetry* in love…"

My'ala paused. A thought came to her, and a cool smile plucked at her cheeks.

"Perhaps that's true," the young girl said.

But I think I know someone who might.

III

THE HEART

Even four years later – where she stood nearly a foot taller with legs like saplings – My'ala still marvelled at the marble-white tree stood stoically at the peak of the hill. In the dying light of evening, the tiny jade leaves seemed to shimmer like fish scales, pinned to the ends of skeletal arms pulling across the plateau towards the sea. The wispy trunk leered left and right with the winds of centuries-past, roots straddling the earth like serpents burrowing for voles. She had not visited that sacred place for months now, she recalled – and knew that, for the mythical gaze of the Sentinel Tree, it was little more than a blink of the eye.

As she crested the hill blanched by the yellow-orange sun, she looked down and smiled at the hunched red robes nestled in the crook of the tree, a length of thin silver chain sliding through his fingers. She stood there for a moment admiring his serenity, pulling the chain in long streaks like the thread of a silk-worm.

Every time I come here, he is even more at peace with the world, she thought. *Part of me wonders if one day he'll simply melt away into the sands: taken away by desert winds and cast far, far away…*

"I was wondering when you would next appear," Artemis the Hermit muttered, not taking his eyes from the chain weaving through his fingers. "It has been some time."

"Five months, I think," she said, dropping into a crouch and setting herself down a few feet from him. "Some time indeed."

"I had no doubt that you would return. And, by the look of you… you have come here with questions to ask."

What? My'ala frowned. "How do you…?" Then realisation hit. "Ah, the tree, of course. I understand. Nothing gets past the Prophets, as ever."

"Nothing gets past the Prophets, indeed," Artemis mused with a smile, turning to her finally. The girl was eclipsed once again by the shimmer of his night-sky eyes, twinkling delicately in the low light like projecting orbs. It seemed to add a depth to his face beyond anything she could reasonably perceive: as if every wrinkle were a cavern and every hair was a forest. An acknowledgement, that this was no ordinary old man sat in the sun under the boughs of a tree.

How mesmerising.

"You know you do something, My'ala, every time you come here," he exclaimed. "The exact same thing."

Do I? "What's that?"

A quiet smile. "You look deep into my eyes, as if you're trying to find something. As if you're searching the depths of night, looking not for something within me, but some-thing within *yourself*. Every time, you do it. And yet you never ask about it."

My'ala shied away, realising she had been read like a book from the very beginning. Cheeks flushing like spilt wine, she made to raise her hand to her face.

"Oh, my dear, it is no problem," Artemis assured her, holding his arm out and waving her hand away. "You likely never felt it right to ask me – as you must admit, it's not every day you see someone with the night sky in their eyes."

"No, it's not..." she mumbled, lifting her gaze again. "So... why *are* your eyes like that?"

The Hermit tilted his grey head away from her for a moment, and studied the vastness of the blue-yellow sky above them. He inhaled slowly, tracing the colours from one cliff-side to the other.

"Because the eyes are a reflection of where we think our answers are," he explained. "It is said that, in the essence of a baby's eyes, there is the permanent reflection of their mother – for that is the one thing they know the most, and where their answers come from. And no matter how far it strays from the coast, a fish's eye reflects the same cove where they were born, for that is where they learnt to survive. It is a simple thing, to reflect and seek our answers; it is something intrinsic to all thinking things. And, in that same way, I am no different. I spend my nights looking up at the vastness and brilliance of the night sky, looking for what guides me there. Because there is something up there, I know... something there that I long to discover, just out of reach. And something I am, after all these years, still trying to find."

"Your eyes reflect the night sky, because it is there you hope to find your answers..." My'ala deduced, nodding her head. "But what answers are there out there? What do you hope to find?"

"I don't know." He seemed almost defeated by the response. "I don't know, and I may never know... but I believe it is out there, somewhere, waiting for someone to find it. And until then, my eyes shall reflect those stars above us, waiting for the day that the answers come."

If there are any to give, that is.

"My sister says there are no answers," My'ala exclaimed. "Or, rather, there are no answers we can know from others – only from within ourselves. She seeks them through her own thoughts."

Artemis raised an eyebrow. "So she doesn't ask questions about her life?"

"In her opinion, if there are no clear answers to our meaning and purpose, then there's no point asking the question at all. She meditates about the day-to-day things... and doesn't think it's any use looking any further than that."

The Hermit considered for a time, then smirked through the roughage of his beard. "Logic dictates that, if no answer reveals itself, then there are no answers. Only *possibilities*. And logic does not deal in the unknown. If the meaning of life is an unknown, then it cannot have meaning."

"You're starting to sound like her."

"Oh, Prophets save us all..."

My'ala laughed, the warmth of the dusk sun swimming across her skin.

"That being said, asking questions with the absence of emotion can often paint the clearest picture," Artemis added, binding the chain around his gnarled hand and holding it still. "Although the answers that then arise, are often as naïve as they are simple."

"Because emotion guides us as much as logic does."

"Exactly."

"Mumma says that my sister doesn't understand the poetry of love. She thinks that her heart and mind are not bound properly, or something like that."

"Is that so? What does your mother believe?"

"That love and care, and the bonds of family are what gives us purpose. That we are inherently looking out for those closest to us in all decisions we make, always."

"Because why would we sacrifice ourselves so callously for someone else, if it was not the most important thing in our lives?"

My'ala looked impressed. "Yes, exactly. She said something very similar to that last we spoke."

"And she has a very good point, in what she says," Artemis admitted, passing the chain to his other hand. "Love is one of the strongest bonds known to us: stronger than the hardest minerals we drag from the mines, even. It is pure and uncompromising. Those guided by it, have a goodness in their hearts that many can only dream of having." He tapped his eyelid. "But love, you see… is also very *blind*."

"Because it's an emotion."

"One of the most potent of them all, in fact. That, and hate. The two are opposites, but both stand atop the same podium. Both are blind, and without thought. So, if you let yourself be guided by either, you will never see clearly again."

"Mumma does not see the desert for the sand."

"Precisely. Because love is a beautiful thing on its own. One of the richest and most incredible feelings there is. To be a mortal without love, is to hardly live at all. It is what sustains us all — everything around us, bound to its power. But… for love to be the meaning of life, when love is blind, is to be led astray by your own heart."

My'ala listened to her own pulse as it rattled through her ears, and felt she understood. "Let love in, but don't let it blind you."

"Very well put. You're starting to sound like a Prophet already!"

She smiled. *One can but dream.*

They sat in silence for some time, on the small hill over-looking the fields, coated in shades of ochre and rust from the distant, fading sun. The sloping landscape before them was patient, unravelling its colours slowly before their very eyes. Yellows and whites bleeding into oranges and browns, and finally the deep, unfathomable crimson red spilling over the plateau like ribbons. It was mesmerising and unstoppable. The delicate shift of day to darkness.

The beauty of nature, before our very eyes.

"So, were neither of them right in their answers?" My'ala asked after a while, turning back to the Hermit.

"Your mother and sister?"

"Yes."

He opened his hands. "Well, think about it: do you feel that either of their answers satisfied the question? Did either of them find the meaning of life?"

"I wouldn't have said so, no. You found fault in both of their answers. My sister, although logical, is naïve for not questioning what could be true. And my mother is guided by her love, but with how blind love can be, it is foolish to let it command you completely."

"Very true on both counts." He looked to her. "But what if I told you your sister and your mother were both different sides of the same coin – that they were both as far away from the truth as the other."

"How?" she pressed. "Surely my mother would be closer, because she at least *entertains* the idea that there's an answer. My sister doesn't even bother."

"Perhaps, yes, but they both miss something crucial in different ways. Your sister, guided by logic, 'will never see the *poetry* of love'. But your mother, attuned to the strength of her love, will never look any further than what's in front of her. Because one is thinking with their mind, and not their heart…"

"And my mother thinks with her heart, not her mind…" My'ala felt the pieces slide into place in her mind, and the mosaic became clearer suddenly. She knew what the Hermit meant. "So it is only if the two are working together, that you can see the true path to the meaning of life."

"Exactly." Artemis nodded like a proud father, the chain between his fingers jangling faintly in the breeze. "You have come a long way from that little girl I first met all those years ago, you know."

She smiled to him. "I have a good teacher."

"You ask the right *questions,* my dear… I am little more

than an old man who thinks too much."

"You don't think too much."

He gestured to the Sentinel Tree. "Try telling that to them…"

She laughed. "Ah, well… the Prophets are fine ones to talk."

"They see something in you, you know, My'ala," Artemis mused. His face seemed to mellow, eyes flitting like shooting stars. "They sense something special within you."

She hid her blushing. "What is it?"

"I have yet to work that out. That, or they keep their truths hidden from me, hoping they will reveal themselves. I'm not sure which it is, but it's… rather *curious,* either way."

"Well, if you do find out…" She stood, acknowledging the angle of the sun over the still blue sea, knowing her dinner would be ready soon. "…do tell me what they have to say."

"That would imply you intend to come here again," the Hermit said, almost hopefully.

My'ala smiled, bowing her head to him. "You have my word, Artemis, I shall return."

"Then I bid you well, my dear, and the Prophets give their blessings." He bowed his head in return. "Until we meet again…"

My'ala turned from him, gazing up at the stoic beauty of the Sentinel Tree one final time before traipsing her way down the slope. Sun-blushed, with the towers and pillars of the City of Arbash rising ahead in shades of hazel, she stopped for a moment and remembered something: an odd question she had been meaning to ask.

"Artemis!" she called out, turning back to the tree. "What was——"

She stopped short, her eyes skimming across the silver roots, up the column of the trunk.

To find the Hermit had gone.

My'ala turned back to the city rising on the plateau just ahead and sighed. *I was meaning to ask, what was that chain you had?*

It looked almost like a pendant...

IV

POWER

One year later…

Boats have appeared out at sea to the west, so the guards say," her father said softly, fingers black with cleaner, wiping a metal rod with a polishing cloth. "Grey sailboats with ten rows of oars. Tattered flags of old cloth billowing in the wind. Every four days or so, one appears just below the horizon, drawing in close to the sea-arch before drifting slowly back to the south. Guards say they've seen the glint of spy lenses from the bow. Has every-one on edge, you know…" Her father stopped suddenly, placing the rod and cloth down. "We have never, in the history of Arbash, encountered another people like us. For those ignorant to possibility, there is the belief that, in the vastness of the desert, we are alone. That there are none other like us. But for people like you or I, Mi-Mi, we know the chances of there being another people like us, in the entirety of the world beyond, is very likely." He tapped his finger on the worktable, drumming until the stone was smooth to the touch. "Which then leaves us with the age old question: what would happen if two different peoples met, having believed they were the only ones in existence? With that sense of supremacy... that *arrogance*. Would they simply come ashore and shake hands, offering trust and peace... or would they come in their droves with their killing weapons, and bring about our end?" A fist, curling and unravelling on the table top. "When I look out on those waters, and see those ships pass by, I ask myself that question every time. But, more than that, I think of our reality, and the fragile nature of life. Because I do wonder if we'll ask for peace or violence in the end... or if we will choose to never ask, and one day it'll be too late to know their answer..."

They stood in the shadowed, open space of her father's workshop, nestled along the outskirts of the Industrial Quarter. My'ala had come down for the day to help with the business and try her hand at it, while also hoping to reconnect with the ageing man as he set about making deals with his machines. To see in him something of the light she had always known. But in that moment, she looked on her father — the person who had guided her through so many challenges in life — and saw there only an old, pained man, exhibiting an emotion she had never seen on his face before. One that made her deeply unsettled.

He's afraid.

He wore the fear in the grey folds of hair coiling around his ears. Wore it in the deep, charcoal-black bands under his eyes. Wore it in the wrinkles like trenches around his mouth and chin. And he wore it, clear as day to her, stood there in his workshop.

And yet, she knew, *he will never admit it.*

Because something has appeared. Something that isn't us, that we don't know. Something that could be here to help us, or harm us. We've never seen ships in the cove before.

What could it mean?

"But I may be jumping at shadows, all the same," her father continued, swelling his chest and reclaiming the metal rod from the table. "The city has had its fair share of... *unusual* encounters. I am sure whoever they are, they are intended for peace – and whatever we choose to do, will be right."

"But you don't believe that, do you, da?" My'ala replied, watching the strength flood from his face almost as quickly as it risen. "You believe something else will happen."

He studied the cylindrical shape in his hands, and tensed his thumbs against the metal. Looking out to the light of the workshop doors just ahead, he bowed his head toward them.

"Walk with me," he said plainly, adjusting his apron. "And let me tell you a thing or two about our true intentions... something about *ruthlessness...*"

They passed through the huge sliding doors, out into the brilliant light of mid-morning sun. My'ala was forced to cover her eyes with her forearm as she emerged, squinting at the buildings and shapes rising up around her. Underfoot, she saw flat-cut rock give way to soft, sandy earth as they moved onto the workshop's courtyard, where her father's farming machines stood on display. Looking up, a high-sided fence of thin columns corralled them, speared at the ends to deter thieves in the night. There were several similar court-yards dotted along the intersecting streets nearby, where other warehouses were and work was no doubt being done. For there was business to be had; deals to be made. And assessing the courtyard around her, and how few machines remained in her father's possession, she couldn't help but smile at the work already done.

He's leagues ahead of his competitors, she thought proudly. *To have a near-empty courtyard is to have a near-full pocket… and that can mean the world to a man like my father.*

Looking up to him with warm eyes, My'ala saw from his expression that he, too, acknowledged the success an empty courtyard brought. She had been there often over the years, offering her help and know-how in exchange for the exper-ience of working in business. And she had seen her father in his lowest ebb many times, struggling to make ends meet, wondering what the future would bring.

And now I see him here, triumphant at last. A youthful vigour returned to his face in that moment, and a deep love filled My'ala's heart. *I couldn't be prouder, da.*

Always.

"They've all been sold, you know," her father said, waving a hand over the remaining machines in the courtyard. "Every last one. Even these small hand ploughs and seed-spreaders have been. I don't think I've ever looked on an empty courtyard in the whole Industrial Quarter… let alone my own." Despite attempts to hide it, there was no doubting his smile. "Never thought I'd see the day."

"It's all come about by your hand, da," My'ala acknowledged. "Believe it to be true, because you're the engineer who made it happen."

He seemed to shy away for a moment, adjusting his apron absently. "Well, I… I did what was necessary to get where I am. I did what any successful businessman does. You make the deals and sell the goods and provide for those who are important to you." Something close to pain echoed in his words. "And the consequences of that, you come to know much later…"

The word lingered in her mind. "What do you mean by *consequences?*"

Her father inhaled guiltily. "What do you know of the business world, Mi?"

"Only the things I've learned from you. How to shake hands with your wrist; how to engage and keep a customer interested; how to clean the machines so they shine well in the sun. That's about all I know, really."

"It's a good start… but that doesn't paint the full picture. That's quite… *romanticised,* for what really goes on."

"And what *does* go on?"

He waved a hand toward the row of small machines that still remained in the courtyard, propped on their stands. My'ala saw the tiny cylinders of the seed-planters and the shovelling coils of the ploughs, knowing from conversations at the dinner-table how both worked and where they were best used.

"So, these are some of the smallest machines that I make in the workshop, and they're typically used for single plots," her father explained, crossing his arms. "I sell one or two a week to new farmers just starting off in the field. And the thing is, those same farmers will come to me time and time again over the next year or so for all their farm-related needs. And they'll do so, purely because they bought this first, tiny machine from me, right at the very beginning. Because there's a trust and reliance there... because the product was good, and they have a good relationship with me. You understand?"

My'ala nodded, looking between the machines and the bearded gaze of her father.

"So, I continue to make the best machines I can, from the best materials I can, for a reasonable price – that way, everyone wins," he continued. "But my competitors, well... they want in on the same market I sell to. They want people to buy their machines over mine. And the only way they can do that, is to better me on one of three things: the quality, the material, or the price. If they do that, the farmers start to look elsewhere... so I have to find a way to manage that."

"Some of those won't benefit you to change, though," My'ala examined. "I mean, if you try and make better machines, you'll take longer to make them, and that's bad for business."

"Very good."

"And if you lower your prices, then you don't make any money yourself..."

"And you, my dear, have seen first-hand what happens when I do that..." A look of guilt trounced his face for a moment, thinking back to their past. "I made many mistakes on the way to where I am now, Mi, that's for sure. Ones that have cost us dearly, I know."

"It's no fault of yours, da. You were doing what you could

to help the business."

"I suppose, yes. But I… well, I just wish it didn't affect the rest of you so much."

"We've recovered, though – we always do, thanks to you." She squeezed his arm. "Besides, I'm here to learn about business, aren't I? There's no time for apologies."

Her father smiled softly. "Very true, Mi… very true."

"So if it wasn't quality and it wasn't price, then that leaves us with the last of them: the materials. That must be how you did it."

"Right you are… and do you know what the machines are made of?"

"Metal, is it not? Iron?"

"A reinforced iron compound, yes – one that seems to form in abundance in the cliffs to the north, in fact. That's why the mines were built there. The garrisons get the bulk of it for their armies, and we get the rest."

"How many mines are there?"

"Oh, dozens. More than I dare to think of."

"And how many produce iron for the farm machines?"

He paused, looking off over the buildings ahead. "Just one."

"Only *one*? Of dozens?" she scoffed in disbelief. "But… that's crazy. Who owns that one?"

Her father let out a sigh of admittance. "I do, Mi."

"*You?*" My'ala scrunched her brow. "How do *you* own it? Why is there only one mine producing iron for the machines?"

"Because that's how I designed it."

"Designed *what?*"

Her father clicked his tongue, exhaling through his nose. "A thing about ruthlessness, Mi," he said measuredly, "is that, no matter how pure of heart you are or intend to be, business can make a monster of you. It will either define you, or it will break you. Now, I sought my meaning in life through farming and machines. And I believed that, if I accumulated enough control over the supplies, I would have enough *power* to provide for my family for the rest of my life. That I would one day be in a position where I am no longer challenged by competitors, and I could protect what I have without fear of losing it, for the remainder of my days. *That* was my belief… and that *became* my purpose."

"Mumma says that love and care and family are what gives us purpose in life," My'ala replied, a knot of emotion in her stomach that she could not unwind.

"They are important, Mi, for certain: I love and care for you, your mother, Dur'al and Su'la more than anything else in this great desert. And even though I know I struggle to say it sometimes, know I would do anything for you four no matter the cost." He levelled his gaze with hers. "But finding *purpose*… now that's very different. Finding purpose in your love and care for others… that only comes when you put it into practice. Because to do so, you must know your limits; you must know what the cost *actually* is to protect those you love. To know just how ruthless you need to be, and how much power you need to keep the waters calm. Love and care cannot do that alone. *That* is where you find purpose."

My'ala looked to the floor, watching heat rise from the sun-baked earth. "How did you do it?" she asked through pursed lips. "How did you finally reach the top?"

Her father exhaled. "A mine shaft collapsed, about eight months ago," he explained. "The entire area was evacuated, deemed too unsafe to mine... but when they did return down there a few days later, they found that an entire new cave system had been exposed, hidden right under their feet for decades. And the council believed that this new cave system was large enough to be classed as a separate mining zone, so the place was put up for auction. When the auction occurred, several prominent bidders were there with a lot of money involved... but with some manoeuvring I managed to secure the zone for myself, out of my own pocket. Damn-well nearly put me out of business, I tell you... but I did it. And then, before anyone could try and squeeze me dry for the minerals that were found there, I made a deal with the council..."

My'ala rolled her eyes. "Let me guess: to amass the iron supply of the Industrial Quarter into a single mining zone, leaving the rest for the army's use. To make things *easier* for them."

"Watch your tone, Mi," her father warned, a stony firmness in his voice. "Remember that I did what was *necessary* to salvage what remained of my business... of the family's income, I might add... and I did so because it was the right thing to do—"

"Why was it? How?"

"Because if I hadn't, someone else *would've*!" Her father, closed his eyes and pinched the bridge of his nose, air billowing from his nostrils like steam. "Because, Mi, if I hadn't bought the mine and secured the supply, then it would've been portioned out on silver plates to every poor fool who thinks they can do the job better — or worse, I would've been squeezed out entirely by more powerful people." He touched a hand to his chest. "*I* did what *I* had to, to control the supply and provide for my family. For you, and ma, and the others."

"At what *cost*, though, da?"

"At the cost that was necessary… for my purpose in this life." A deep sadness at the corners of his lips. "And that cost, Mi, is one that I bear like a black cloud every single day." He waved a hand out across the surrounding buildings and adjacent courtyards nearby. "You see all of these other workshops, next to mine?"

She nodded, eyes jumping between them.

"All of them were once used to build farming machines. We four here were the main players in the market, at the time. We had a good laugh, competing against one another. But, one by one, they all fell… until I was the only one who remained. In control of supply, production, distribution… all of it. I *own* the farming business now… and I put all of them out of business. And now I stand alone, at the top of a pillar surrounded by nothing but dust, wondering what the cost really was." He sighed, shaking his head. "You and your ma used to be so proud of what I had accomplished, in finally finding this success. And for a moment, when we left the workshop, I saw it again in your eyes: that hopeful, beautiful pride. It was nice to feel that my success here *meant* something, even if just for a moment. But now… now that I've laid the truth of it out to you, I can see that there's none of that left: nothing of the pride left in you. And *that*… is the true nature of power and business. That is the cost of my purpose here. You do what you must to be the hero, but will always become the villain in the end…"

My'ala closed her eyes, and felt the heat wash across her scalp. A solemn, broken weight fell across her shoulders, and everything seemed suddenly darker.

The cost of it, she thought in despair. *People's livelihoods, ruined because of my father's choice. My own life, held aloft at their expense. That my father went against his own morals to pursue a meaning of life that he neither wanted nor felt comfortable with. Ruthlessness, he says. Power and business…*

And was it really worth it, in the end? She sighed, meeting her father's despondent eyes. *You were in a job, and money was fragile, and you had a choice — you found control, provided for us, and did what any other person would have in your position. That was the cost of what we have… of everything in our lives now. That was your purpose… and it saved us.*

And I know you are not a cruel man, father… not in the world of business, she concluded. *You are far more than that, to me.* My'ala found it in her to smile.

You're a survivor.

"You'll never be a villain to me, da," she exclaimed. "You did what was necessary for those you care about. Your pursuit of control, and what it cost, was just part of that process. You found meaning, in reaching that place. Not because of a fixed thing like love… but because of what you knew you had to do. I can't demonise you for that. How could I, for what you've done for us?" He held his arm. "You're still my da… that never changes. And in your own way, despite the despair you feel… you're still a hero, too."

Her father — his face opening up with a wonderful glow —

opened his hands out to her and embraced her tightly in his arms. My'ala embraced him in return, face pushing against his chest like she used to when she was a child, where the *thrum* of his heartbeat echoed in her ears. Her father looked down for a moment and kissed her on the forehead, stroking her hair with his huge, calloused hands.

"Thank you, Mi," he said slowly, voice quivering. "And I'm sorry. Truly, I'm sorry."

"Don't be," she replied, stepping back. "You're still my da, and I still love you all the same."

He nodded, blinking through the glassy sheen coating his eyes. "But you see, now, from what has happened, why I am so unsure of the newcomers who trace our waters, and what their intentions are. I have seen — *felt* — what the pursuit of power does to people. Because people are cruel and ruthless and will tear everything apart for what they desire. The business world reflects people's worst intentions. And the ideas of conquest, they… they are not too dissimilar." He placed a hand on her shoulder, steadying her nerves. "So, if you see boats out there on the waves, or hear talk of *peace* and *amnesty* in the streets around you, remember what you have seen and heard here today. Because if we aren't ready to stand and face them if the worst happens, then the answers we seek will not be with our words…"

A call to attention chimed somewhere behind him.

"… they will be at our *throats*."

Her father pulled away, squeezing her shoulder, and turned toward the voice who had called him, approaching the outer walls of the courtyard with gate keys in his hand — leaving My'ala stood in the open blinking slowly, looking off to the west.

Peace and amnesty, she muttered within, her heart in her throat. *Cruelty and ruthlessness. Business. The pursuit of power. Conquest.*

The word sent chills up her spine, as if the thin columns of the courtyard were closing in all around her.

Is what my father says really true? Are we really facing such odds? Her head spun, the cresting sun above her drenching the streets with light. *Are people really as cruel and power-hungry as he says? It can't be, surely. It can't be that bad I don't know. I don't... know...*

She drew sharp breaths through her lips, holding her hands out as if she were about to fall.

I don't know what to do. What should I believe?

I have to find Artemis.

V

THE VISIONLESS

Despite the midday heat, My'ala ran most of the distance between the city gates and the Sentinel Tree, skipping down rocky steps and skirting past groves of grape and clementine with her heart pulsing in her head. As she reached the small hill and started to ascend, the pearlescent branches of the ancient tree seemed to bend low towards her, sensing the air like tendrils. They shared the burden of her unease for a moment, the tiny jade leaves whispering among themselves — turning to the old man in the burgundy robes nestled between their roots, a chain pulling between his fingers.

Hoping he would have the answers, and set still My'ala's soul.

"Artemis!" she cried.

The Hermit turned to her as she approached him, and appeared concerned at the trembling in her hands. "What's wrong, my dear?" he said softly. "What's happened?"

My'ala stopped, catching her breath, half-collapsing into a nook of the tree near the old Hermit's spot. She sat back and lay her head against the cracked bark, closing her eyes for a moment to think.

"It's the middle of the day," Artemis added. "You don't usually come this early."

"I was with my father…" she rasped in reply, drawing air through her nose and out through her mouth. "I was meant to be helping him all day at his workshop, helping with his machines… but then something happened. I feigned that I was ill and that I couldn't stay, so he said for me to go home and rest. But I couldn't rest, not after what he said… I had to come here and speak with you and the Prophets and the tree. I had to know the truth."

"What truth, young girl?"

Her eyes traced down the rows of farmland toward the sea-arch at its base, a knot in her throat as she did so. She scanned over the distant waters of the cove for signs of moving shadows — of the enemy her father had warned of — but found nothing of it there. Nothing but calm blue waves, and an unnerving fear in her heart.

"Have you seen boats out there, on the waves?" She betrayed all emotion, speaking plainly as if nothing were wrong. "There have been a few reports of unknown ships out in the cove. I just wondered what you knew about it."

"Oh yes, I have seen them." He nodded. "Tiny shadows like birds, drifting along the horizon to the south. They come every few days, so the Prophets tell me – but who they are or what they want, we do not know."

"So it is true…"

"What's true?"

"What do you think they want from us?" she pleaded. "Why do you think they come past this way and enter the cove?"

"We cannot know what they want from us. We've never seen them before."

"But why do they come here? Why do they observe us?" There was a franticness in her voice that made the Hermit frown.

"They are probably just as curious as we are of them. Trying to work out what we are, and what our intentions are. Are we friend or foe, ally or threat… that kind of thing."

"But what if there's more than that? What if they want to attack us? I… I mean we don't know. We don't know anything. What if we're in danger? What if they think we're their enemies—"

"*My'ala*," Artemis spoke firmly.

The young girl seemed to shrink at the sound of her name, wary of his tone of voice. Realising, with hindsight, how hysterical she sounded – *how I've let my emotions get the better of me.*

"My'ala, my dear, why are you asking these questions?" he inquired softly. "What has caused you this profound anxiety?" The old man spoke with a deep care in his voice, which dissipated her fears to little more than a shallow stream. She shook her head and shrugged.

"I don't know, really. I… I was with my father earlier,

and he was talking about the ships in the cove. He said about how strange it was. How we've never seen anything like it. He was talking about the city, and our people, and our way of life… and I saw that he was genuinely afraid of what comes next." She sucked her lips together. "I've never seen my father afraid before, and… and it *terrified* me. So I took myself away from it all, because I don't know what to do or what to make of it or anything. The things he said about people, and about business and our purpose… they felt so abhorrent. I just didn't know what to do…"

"It's okay, My'ala, you're perfectly within your right to feel uneasy about these things… what did your father say about it?"

"He said that… business was a reflection of people's worst intentions. That it was cruel and ruthless, and made people into monsters. It's why he's so cynical about people all the time. But he also believes that there is a purpose there, too: a drive and a passion to work hard and do your best and provide for those who are important to you. Or something like that…"

"Your father likes the meaning of life to be practical."

"He is a very practical man."

"He takes pride in his work?"

She paused. "He does, although he holds a lot of shame too. Shame for the people who have been put out of business because of him, or squeezed out by his actions. He questions whether it was worth it."

"And was it worth it, for him, do you know?"

My'ala shrugged. "He's of the belief that, if he didn't claim the power for himself, then someone else would've.

And if it meant that we could be happy and prosperous for the rest of our lives, then it will always be worth the cost of putting others under."

"Preservation of your own, at the expense of others." The Hermit considered. "Very interesting..."

"My father thinks the worst of people," My'ala said quietly with something verging on despair. "He knows family, and he knows what he can trust – and everything outside of that, he cautions against. He sees other people not for who they are, but by what agenda they potentially have..."

She looked to Artemis for any reaction to her words, studying the moonlit expanse of his eyes for any shimmer of thought. But he seemed to do nothing, transfixed to the distant horizon ahead of them, shrouded in his robe – the only motion being the tiny silver chain twisting around his fingertips, like a silk worm dancing through caves.

How strange...

"What is that chain that you have?" she asked suddenly. "I remember seeing it before the last rain came, and I meant to ask about it... but I haven't seen you with it since then. I've only just remembered. It looks like a pendant..."

Artemis smiled. "It is indeed a pendant, My'ala – very observant of you," he replied, holding it up to the sun. "And in answer to your question, well... I don't actually know what this chain is. I know what it *symbolises*, of course, as a pendant... but why it is here, or why the tree offers it to me sometimes, I cannot fathom."

"Wait, the tree *offers it* to you?"

"Yes... rather unusual, isn't it?" With his free hand, the Hermit pointed to a low-hanging branch just above their heads. "It dangles there, sometimes, just before you appear. As if the tree has revealed some of its secrets to us, through the silver coils of this chain. I have been here countless rains over what feels like an eternity, waiting for the Prophets to offer a sign. And it would appear, young My'ala... that the sign they gave, was this pendant connected to you."

"So it only appears when I come to this tree?" She felt a vacuum open in her chest. *How can it possibly know?*

"Not always, no... it appears only very occasionally, usually when you have some revelation you wish to disclose, or we talk of life's greater meaning."

"And is that what the pendant symbolises?"

"See for yourself."

In the cresting sun, with the rolling cliffs stretching out across the valley in the distance, My'ala's gaze fell upon the tiny silver shape at the base of the chain. She looked at it for some time, trying to make sense of what it meant; of what it was trying to show her. A tiny, curved piece of metal, no bigger than a button.

"It's a crescent moon," she exclaimed. "But... what does that tell us about the meaning of life? It's... I don't understand what I'm meant to see here."

"That's because it holds different meaning to everyone, my dear," the Hermit replied, lowering it back into his palm. "What I see within its tiny form, will be entirely different to what you will see in it."

"And what do you see in it?"

Artemis made a contemplative inhale of breath, and closed his fingers around the pendant. "The crescent moon, by my understanding, is the natural reflection of purity and the soul: curling in on itself, almost like an embrace, to shelter what lies inside. And we, as mortals, have an expression of that same purity, similar to the shape of a crescent moon: that of a new-born child. When a child lies within its mother's womb, or curls up to sleep softly in the night, it will do so by tucking in on itself, cradling itself, almost by instinctive." He nodded. "And a child, by nature, is the purest form of humanity. They have not been influenced by the world; they have not made choices nor experienced their consequences. There is no good or bad in the existence of a child — they are simply here to be. And because of that, in both the crescent moon and the new-born child, the soul that they cradle is the purest that we can comprehend. And so in turn, I believe, nestled within that crescent shape in the night sky above, the answers to the meaning of life must also reside."

"So you look at the night sky... because you're trying to interpret the essence of the moon itself?" My'ala deduced, scanning the blue high above.

"Yes, precisely."

"But if you're looking for the meaning of *our* essence, then why look at a crescent moon? Why not a child?"

"Because of our mortal nature, My'ala." He placed a hand against his chest. "Because what makes a child so pure, is that they are the unquestioned origin of all things. They are without influence, so to speak. So if I were to find a child, and ask them of their meaning in life... I would be breaking that purity of the soul, just by being there and asking the question. Not that they would know how to answer such a question, anyway... as a matter of fact, I'm still surprised you do, after all these years."

"I've always been beyond my years," she said proudly.

Artemis smiled. "That you have, my dear... that you have."

"So, if that's the case... what answer does the moon offer you?"

"The purest one... because the great thing about the night sky is, no matter how many questions you ask of it, it will never change. It is always infinite, and everlasting."

"And whatever answer it gives, therefore, is... *'the'* answer."

"Precisely. And that is not something you can obtain of your own accord. There's too much influencing a mortal mind to give a *pure* answer. And *that* is why I look to the stars – and the stars reflect back into me."

My'ala caught a glimpse of his eyes for a moment, and felt her heart jump. *Perhaps the moon's purity is rubbing off on you.*

Perhaps he's closer to the 'true' answer than he realises.

"Although, I'm glad that you've asked after the pendant," Artemis added, turning to her. "It is actually quite pertinent to our conversation about your father, and about the ships in the cove to the west."

Something in My'ala's chest sunk at the reminder of what lay just off their shores – a trepidation built within her that drew sweat across her palms.

"How so?" she asked.

"Because your father... well, he forgets what humanity is, at its core. He forgets that every one of us begins from a point of utter purity, and is only then tainted by the environment around us. We are products of our growth, of course – but every one of us has, deep within, that same purity that was cradled within us as a child. Your father finds purpose in his work, and regards others cynically – but in doing so, he denies them the chance to show their good sides." He leaned over to her to whisper. *"Maybe, because he's lost sight of his own..."*

My'ala considered, and nodded her head in agreement. "My father feels a lot of shame for what he's done to get where he is. For how many others he's put under, to give us the life we have. And maybe that shame is clouding his hope, and in turn making it seem like everyone else is bad too..."

"One of the first emotions we feel, as mortals, is despair: from the very first time we want something, and are told we cannot have it. Because we despair what life cannot give us – but perhaps we should instead be more grateful about what life *has* given us."

"To count our blessings."

"No," he corrected: "to make our blessings *count.*"

My'ala thought for some time on the Hermit's words, looking off to the distant olive groves spilling down the valley. The sun and the wind danced across their tiny leaves to make it look as if they were waving: a thousand tiny hands rippling over and through each other. It brought a steadiness to her pulse, challenging the rises of fear that threatened to pull her down. She closed her eyes for a moment and let the heat of the sun blanche her face – and she could have sworn, in the air above, that the tiny jade leaves whispered her name.

"I best be going soon," she said eventually, opening her eyes. "It's getting close to high-sun."

"Of course, my dear — I imagine your mother is wondering why you aren't home yet," Artemis replied.

"That's very true."

"But, before you do go, I will say this." He raised his hands up, letting the silver chain hang between them with the crescent moon at its centre. "Whenever you next find yourself lost, or asking questions that seem far too big to comprehend, find a quiet place and look up to the stars for me. Ask your questions to the night sky, and reconnect with that deepest, purest part of you that resides within your soul — the tiny piece of the new-born you still have left. And you will find, I hope, that the answers shall come to you like a wash of rain, and your mind shall be clear once again." A pause. "Maybe even invite your father too, if he's willing… I'm sure he has a number of questions he wants answering."

She looked off to the City of Arbash atop the high plateau to their right. "Perhaps I will… perhaps I will." She stood and brushed herself off, turning to him with a polite smile. "Thank you, Artemis. I feel far more settled than I was."

"My pleasure, My'ala," he replied, bowing. "And remember: when you look down to the cove and see the ships there, and fear for the worst, do not lose that hope that things will be okay. Because although time changes, and lives change with it, the uncertainty of today is the clear air of tomorrow. Never forget that."

She looked back down to the aquamarine sea — down the valley to the painted cove far below — and drew in a long, warm breath.

I won't.

VI

DUTY

Four months later...

My'ala heard the buckling of straps and the hushed, biting remarks of her parents, and knew the fate that awaited them long before she even entered her brother's room. Crossing the landing slowly, with a deep anxiety tickling in her chest, My'ala's heart wound tighter as she approached the smudged image of the crow on his door. And all she found the strength to do, was sigh.

Part of her had known the day would come, ever since she had first laid eyes on the grey sails out at sea. Ever since the first whispers of fear had glided down their city streets. My'ala had known, and she had sensed it gnaw away at her thoughts for months gone past with nothing to show for it.

But part of her had hoped, in that same breath, that something would stop that ball rolling. That maybe fate had some other plan for her dear brother, consumed by his self-declared destiny. Perhaps he would see sense; perhaps he would see the consequences inflicted on his family, and reconsider. Such were the thoughts that had come to her, in her moments of quiet hope.

But they were thoughts that were dashed almost as quickly as they had sprung, when she opened the door and saw the short-sword lying on his bed.

And knew fate had decided for her.

My'ala stood for some time and stared at the weapon, unsure what to make of it. She had seen a sword before, she knew: swords that were held in the scabbards of the city guards, stood idle in their barracks or pacing along the vast walls. She had even seen one used, once: drawn against a thief in a marketplace, the blade striking out toward their hand. The thief had escaped with a graze across their wrist and a loaf of bread to show for their efforts, but she had always regarded swords as something *other people* had. Be it an axe in the hands of a palace guard, or the knife tucked in the folds of a merchant's robe, it had been something that had existed only on the very edge of her orbit – something she had little contact with in reality.

So to see one strewn across a bed in her own house, with the intended purpose of spilling blood, made My'ala both intensely curious and sick with dread.

This can't be, she thought, shuddering.

Are they really out there?

The door peeled open a fraction more, and in the half-light of the room she locked eyes with her father and stifled a gasp. He was frightening pale, stood hunched with eyes like turrets, the steel round of a shoulder-plate clasped in his tired hands. She had never seen him like that before, and a broken fear ate at her mind at the sight. The look he gave her was almost a plea, in that moment, as she continued to push the door wider and finally laid eyes on her brother.

Strapped head-to-toe in a suit of armour.

"What do you think, Mi?" Dur'al boasted, posing. "Quite impressive, wouldn't you say?"

My'ala did not usher a word, her eyes passing from the brown-orange sash across his neck and shoulders to the supremely-polished caps of his steel boots. A bulb of sickness built in her stomach with such force that she placed a hand there to steady it. *He looks like a soldier,* she muttered within. *My own brother.*

Why?

"Go easy on her, Dur'al," her father said, pulling the boy's shoulder down to attach the plate. "I imagine she's quite shocked to see you like this."

"You're overthinking things, da," he retorted. "She just isn't used to me looking so smart, I'm sure!"

My'ala produced a half-smile, shrugging her shoulders.

Dur'al threw his hands up. "See! I told you."

Her father met her eyes again as he adjusted the final strap — and he saw the lie across her lips without so much as blinking. My'ala rolled her tongue.

Is it that obvious?

"What are you going out to do, Dur'al?" she asked quietly, pressing her fingers together.

"Well, I'm doing what I've always wanted to do," her

brother replied plainly, rolling his shoulder to see if the plate stayed in place. "I'll be raising my sword and wearing the Arbash crest with pride. I'll be doing my duty to the city and its people."

"And what is that?"

"I'll be in the rear-guard of the regiment that will march down to the cove and send those invaders back to whence they came."

Her heart seemed to stop.

"They're *here?*" she scoffed. *It can't be…*

"A few days ago, six ships landed in the cove beneath the sea-arch, drifting silently to shore," her father explained, standing back and gazing out the window. "They came under the cover of night – the guards stationed along the walls only knew they were there by the flicker of their torches. The ships remained there until the early break of dawn before they finally cast off, leaving behind three large camps and an estimated hundred soldiers setting up posts along the shore-line…"

"Wait, *soldiers?*"

"People with swords and grey-armoured coats. Some of the guards saw them sparring this morning, so the reports say." He sighed and shook his head. "The ships that have scouted the cove for the past few months, were in fact spies, and it seems that they've been planning an invasion of Arbash the entire time. And we have done *nothing* to prevent it, and nothing to prepare… just as I predicted, when we first saw them…"

"And it seems like I was right to keep a few recruitment books back," Dur'al interrupted, waving one hand toward her. "I mean, it's better to be prepared and know what you're doing for these things, especially when the worst happens."

She watched her father as he made no acknowledgement of Dur'al's words — but did catch the shadow of his jaw clench in the sun. She gulped.

This is bad.

"What happens from here?" My'ala inquired, trying to make sense of what was happening as her mind spiralled ever deeper.

"I'll be called up by the Marshal just after high-sun, along with any other recruits looking to join, and we will congregate in the town square by the palace," he said. "We will have a short assessment of our skills, to work out who is needed where, and then we will be sent out the west gate to join the city guard in their camp. And because of my *lacklustre and inexperienced* fighting style" — he scowled toward their father — "I will likely be placed in the rear-guard to reinforce if things go bad."

"That sounds like the safest place to be."

"It is... but I can't do my duty as a fighter if I don't then actually *fight*."

"Testament to the soldiers' merit if you don't need to be engaged. Sounds like the best-case scenario to me."

Dur'al pursed his lips and produced little more than a grunt in response — and just out of sight, she couldn't help but notice her father's proud smile.

A glimmer of the man I once knew.

"It doesn't matter where I am," Dur'al said defiantly, waving his hand. "I'll still get stuck in where I can. It's something I've always wanted to—"

Footsteps crossed the landing behind My'ala, like the heavy breach of a landslide, and shivers crept up her spine. Suddenly she was being moved aside, her sister's hands pulling through the door and standing between them all, a venomous snarl curling over her face.

The heat of the room rose with the blink of an eye.

"What do you want?" Dur'al spat.

"I wondered if it was true, that you were finally going to the army…" Su'la said bitingly. "And then I heard our own mother weeping in the garden, eyes red-raw… and I *knew* you'd made that choice."

"Mother has a lot going on, Su'la. It isn't just about this. Her stomach's acting up…"

"Yea, I can imagine she's quite *sick* at the moment."

"Look, she has her own stuff to deal with about all of this. It isn't just because of this. Because if you haven't realised – while locked away in your room studying how people think, letting the world slip into chaos just outside – there are actual *enemy soldiers* in the cove to the west, within marching distance of this very house. You don't think that's playing on her mind too?"

"Perhaps it is, yes. Playing on a lot of people's minds I imagine. But what I don't think she really *needs* on top of that, is to grieve her only son as he marches off to fight, because he may as well already be *dead!*"

"Su'la, please," their father interrupted, lifting his hand to her shoulder. "Let's not fight about this…"

Su'la swatted the hand aside. "And *you*… where has your backbone gone, huh? Where has that defiant strength gone, keeping this family together, averting crises before they happen. Because your son is walking headlong into one, and you're stood here looking like a ghost playing dress up!"

"Dur'al has made his decision – although it goes against my wishes, and those of the family, we can do nothing about it. If his future lies in the defence of this city… then that is where it lies."

"What happened to *'no-one under my roof shall ever enter the army'*? He's only seventeen rains old! He's barely an adult, and you think he can decide between life and death like that?" She scoffed. "This doesn't just affect him. This affects everyone in the house. I don't want to lose my brother; ma doesn't want to lose her son. His *actions"* – she speared a finger at Dur'al accusingly – "will hurt this family forever, if he goes through with this. Why don't you stop him, da?"

Her words came out desperately, voice crackling. Knuckles tensed by her side. Like a guilty prisoner sentenced before the court, their father lowered his eyes to the floor and sighed.

None of them want this, My'ala thought, stuck in the middle of it all. *Su'la is furious – ma is heartbroken – and father is lost.*

I don't know what to do.

"Da doesn't stop this," Dur'al grumbled, "because he sees why I do it."

"Oh yea? And why is that?" Su'la replied.

"Because I don't just do this for myself. My recruitment to the army – going out there and facing the enemy – is not because I'm headstrong or prideful or any of that. This isn't about the family, Su'la. In many ways, it isn't even about me." He gestured to the open window. "There is an entire city out there, full of people: rich and poor; workers and business-people; merchants and blacksmiths and bakers. A diverse and wonderful city that we call home. And every single one of those people, from whatever walk of life they come from... they are *afraid* of what lurks at the bottom of the valley. Afraid for their lives, and their families, and their friends. They're afraid that the world will unravel before their very eyes, and there's nothing that they can do to stop it. It's despairing."

"And what difference does that make to you?"

"Because my purpose in life, Su'la, is to serve others. It is my *duty* to do what I can for this city and its people — to protect them and care for them and strive for the greater good in all this. I pride myself in my commitment to the service of others: it's why I admire what ma does, serving on the council. She does what she can for the good of the many, every single day, and... and recruiting to the army, in the city's time of need... that's just my way of doing that. Because there is a *very real* threat out there, with the intention of invading this city. We don't know what they'll do to us — and I'm not waiting around to find out either."

He turned then to their father, head stooped like a widow at a funeral, and Dur'al placed a hand on his shoulder.

"I don't resent you, da, for keeping me away from the army for so long," the boy said softly. "I know why you did it: because you wanted to protect me, and you didn't want me to be consumed by the arrogance of service. And, before the ships were sighted in the cove... well, I had come to agree with you." He sighed. "But you know, as much as I do, that I cannot stand idle while an enemy rallies against us."

He turned back to his sisters. "And one day, I hope you two will see that as well. Until then, all I can ask is for your forgiveness, and to pray to the Creator for my safety."

My'ala stood in the doorway, the air thick with her brother's words — so tangible she could almost taste them. She felt pinned to the doorframe, her heart through the floor, an emptiness in her legs that made it difficult to walk.

A duty to protect all of us... a meaning found in things far greater than ourselves, she thought, almost ready to collapse. *He joins up regardless of our feelings, because it is not our feelings in the end that matter: it's for the good of all people. To march out and raise the banner and look death in the eye...*

All in the name of duty.

My'ala stood back and watched as her speechless sister shook her head and paced back out of the room, muttering curses under her breath.

Then in turn, her insular father turned to his only son and patted him across the collar, passing a reserved smile before leaving the room and disappearing down the stairs.

And My'ala stood for some time, watching Dur'al admire himself in his armour, rubbing the steel plates with an odd piece of cloth to keep them looking polished and new. He was completely absorbed in his own space, transfixed to his image in the reflection and the young girl found herself slowly fade from his interest.

Placing a hand around the lip of the door, she muttered a prayer and drew it closed, levelling her eyes with the crow for a moment.

Hearing the squawk of her heartbroken mother just outside.

VII

THE FOOLISH

Looking up to the Sentinel Tree stood proudly at the peak of the hill – and terrified of looking west for fear of what she may see in the cove – My'ala closed her eyes and sighed.

Why am I here?

She had steeled herself against her emotions, when she had left Dur'al's room. All she had wanted to do was scream at him: to tell him he was wrong; that his beliefs were wrong; that he was hurting them with his actions. She had wanted to challenge him, and show him the error of his ways as Su'la had tried to. Hoping he would change his mind. Wishing, on some distant star, that the world didn't have to be that way.

But instead she had pulled the door closed, studying the

crow painted on his door, acknowledging that it was futile to try and convince him otherwise. Because his actions were ones akin to his very soul — and to ask him to go against that, for the sake of his family, was asking him to lose himself.

Not something I'm willing to do.

So she had gone instead to her mother, sat weeping in the garden. Approaching her in silence, she knelt under the shade of the huge hibiscus tree, the golden hummingbirds perched on nearby branches with their heads bent in mourning. My'ala wrapped her arms about her mother, who clung to her in return as if it were life or death. She let no emotion rise, but sensed her mother calm as she squeezed tighter, until one tiny sentiment trickled from her mouth like a quiet stream and the tree seemed to engulf them altogether.

"He's doing what he believes is right... and for that I'm proud of him."

But why? she had longed to cry out, as they parted ways and My'ala returned to her bedroom to meditate. *You're sat weeping, ma... how can you possibly be proud?* She tried to reason with it, inhaling deeply through her nose, but found no answers rise within her. There was only silence, and city streets, and the distant sun blaring through her window. *And the old Hermit beneath the Prophet's Tree, somewhere in the beyond.*

The one with all the answers...

Drawing back to reality, My'ala braced herself and ascended the small hill. She sensed the air shift around her almost immediately; heard the distinct rustle of branches as the ancient boughs above stooped low to greet her. As she reached its peak, she lifted her gaze and was shocked to find

Artemis was already looking to her, the night stars in the rounds of his eyes glistening softly at her approach.

He seems older, she concluded, studying his bony fingers and how his eye sockets seemed to protrude significantly like an owl's. *Or perhaps this is a reflection, like he said.*

Perhaps I am now older too.

"I wasn't planning to come here," My'ala admitted, making to sit. "I wasn't sure if——"

Artemis said nothing – instead, he waved his hand, wanting her to stay standing. She stood puzzled for a few moments, until the old Hermit raised his hand to clasp against the bark of the tree at his side, and slowly lifted out of the roots to his feet.

He moved incredibly slowly, with twitches seizing down his legs. Every fibre in his body seemed to groan with pain. She had never seen him move before, and almost winced at the sheer exhaustion he faced just stretching his knees out beneath the robes.

And then he lost his grip suddenly, and looked ready to fall. My'ala swept across the dry earth like a skating bird, pulling an arm under his shoulder to keep him steady. She held him aloft, bristling at how little of his body there was beneath the huge burgundy robes, and helped him rise to a full stand and push away from the tree.

"You're not well," My'ala deduced, surprising herself with the weight of sadness that bloomed suddenly in her chest.

Artemis, craning his neck like a vulture to observe the world beyond, nodded his head slowly. "It is true, I am not well," he muttered. "A life of thinking beneath this tree has taken its toll on me, it seems."

"What's happening to you?"

Oddly, he smiled. "I'm dying, My'ala. I am, after all, incredibly old – far older than any one person you've ever known in this world. And, like all mortal beings of this blessed place… there is a time when that comes to an end."

What? No…

My'ala's legs became incredibly weak beneath her. She tightened her jaw, fighting the tears that swelled to the surface. "But… you can't die yet… you haven't found your answers. The meaning of life, the purpose of all things, I… you can't *die…*"

"The answers of our forebears – those that we seek – are not always forthcoming, my dear. The truths we hope to find, do not always reveal themselves until the end… or sometimes not at all." A shift in his robes, indicating a shrug. "We just make the most of what we know, and the time that we have."

"But I *need* you, Artemis!" My'ala pleaded. "I don't know the answers. I don't know what to do… what to make of my life. Everything is changing, and I… I have nowhere else to go."

Like a crane upon the salt-flats, the Hermit lifted the wing of his robe and placed it on her shoulder. "Then tell me what is wrong, my dear. Let us carry on as if nothing has changed. We should make the most of this time, after all."

She grit her teeth, nearly chewing through her tongue with the force of it, and sighed.

Be strong.

"My brother has enlisted to join the army," she muttered

slowly, painfully. "As we speak, he's going to be assessed by the Marshal, and sent to the field camp just beyond the western walls. In the coming days, he'll likely clash swords with the newcomers, and… well, I fear he may not survive to come home and tell the tale."

"I recall you saying that he has always aspired to be a soldier."

"Yes, ever since I was born. And he was nearly going down a different path – as of a few months ago, he had almost accepted he would never join the army – but once the ships landed in the cove, the decision for him was clear." She shook her head. *Why does it have to be like this…*

"And why did he choose to join, in the end?"

My'ala clicked her tongue. "Duty. He joined because he believed it was his duty to serve and protect the city and its people. Against our wishes, he has chosen to serve."

Artemis dragged a hand through his grey beard. "Your brother seems to possess a stubborn selflessness that even an old fool like me could hardly contend with…"

The young girl snorted, appreciating the reprieve.

"That being said, what your brother has done is not inherently wrong. And it is an unsurprising course, when you consider the views of your parents."

"What do you mean?"

"Well, if I'm remembering correctly, your mother acts with love and care, and does whatever she can for those closest to her. Your father does the same, but in a more practical sense: no matter the cost, he will provide for you all, even when forced to reconcile with less savoury acts. Your *brother,* therefore, is a mix of the two: no matter the cost, and in the way he can do the most good, he will protect and care for you and the people of Arbash, and do so with the same love he holds for his own family." He nodded, smiling. "Because duty, you see… is love in motion."

"But I was always told that our beliefs are shaped by our lives… by how we're raised, and what we learn?"

"And a lot of it is just that, yes." Artemis placed a hand against his chest. "But remember that we also share the essence of our parents, too. We were once one and the same. Perhaps we interpret the world in the way that we do, because that is how our mothers and fathers do so — only we draw different conclusions."

My'ala puzzled at the Hermit's words. *Strange… I had never thought of it like that.* "So my brother has chosen duty… using the same beliefs as my parents?"

"They were one and the same once, My'ala. Remember that." He nodded. "It is why you are all so different — why you think so different, despite being of the same blood. It is why you don't understand your brother's choices; it's why you struggle with what your father has done. It's why you come here, most of all. Because you don't just want to understand *how* they think: you want to know *why* they value it too." He gestured to the tiny jade leaves above. "It's no wonder the Prophets admire you so much."

A warmth in her heart, like the heat of a gojan fruit on an empty stomach. She looked across the porcelain bark beside her and smiled.

I rather admire you too.

"How does his decision make you feel?" Artemis asked her suddenly, drawing her attention back.

"It makes me feel… *despairing.* Upset. Confused, mostly."

"Because you could never think to make that decision?"

"I am not someone for the army by my nature: the army is a place for tough people with tough hearts. I don't have that. But even then, neither does my brother. That's the bit I don't understand."

"He does not have a strong heart?"

"Well he… he does, I suppose, because he cares a lot."

"So what makes him not a '*tough person*'?"

"I… well, I don't know."

"Strength is to show you care, and know it isn't weakness. If your brother is willing to put his life on the line for duty, he doesn't strike me as a weak person."

"That's true, but he still doesn't seem like he'd be in the *army.* Why would he be in the army?" she spat, almost insulted by the idea. "Why can't he be a blacksmith or a cook or a sooth-sayer or a damn *farmer* for all I care. Why choose the army? Can't he be dutiful in some other way, and not put his life at risk?"

Artemis clasped his hands together against his chest, and sighed at the question. "It cannot be so."

"But why?"

"Because duty is not a fixed purpose. True duty, if one finds their meaning in it, is as the river runs. Your brother finds duty in the most pressing needs – that which affects the most people. Maybe when money is tight, it is a merchant; maybe when food is low, it is a farmer. But right now, with soldiers and supply tents in the bay just below us… there is only one duty that matters, really. And that is to stand and fight." He levelled his gaze, sensing the sadness in her heart.

"I'm sorry that you and your family are undergoing so much stress because of his choices, My'ala. It can be no easy thing to go through. Your brother, although dismissive and proud, is no fool. He loves you all dearly, and cares for you deeply – he loves his way of life, and the things that make it worth living. And he knows that these newcomers… whoever they are… *they* are the threat to all that. And not just for him, but for all people." His gaze drifted out toward the sea. "You say you want your brother to be a blacksmith, or a cook… to work within the safety of the walls, away from the derision of the army. I understand that, and I'm sure he understands that too. But just remember, your brother may be fighting in the army so that he *can* have a safe job once this is over. Because if they win, it's not just his future that gets thrown into chaos: it's everyone's. Your whole collective way of life will be swept up from under you. So, despite the despair and anguish you feel in your chest – and rightly so… remember that he's doing this so your father can keep his business; your mother can stay on the council; your sister can continue with her studies. So that *you* can have a job one day too, even."

"Because that's what duty is…" My'ala muttered, a sombre acceptance pulling in her heart. *That's what duty is.* She searched deep within herself, and despite the Hermit's words something inside still refused to accept her brother's reasons for enlisting. It still felt like a sleight; it still stung whenever she thought of the sword led dormant on his bed.

But then, part of her understood that maybe she wasn't *meant* to understand. That she wasn't meant to agree with his choice. *Because we are not the same person… nor guided by the same beliefs,* she surmised. *I, like my family, will never be content with what he has chosen to do, but that also then doesn't matter. He does it because he cares, and because that's how he shows it. All we have to do is accept that.* A quivering breath escaped her throat.

And pray he comes home.

"Do you think he'll be safe?" she asked.

"Perhaps the stars above us know, but no mortal can answer that question for you, my dear," Artemis said simply. "All we can do is wish, and pray, and hope that he and the others shall prevail. Because that's all it is in the end: hope. Hope, and a matter of time…"

My'ala nodded, and finally found the courage to look down to the cove in the valley beneath them. To finally lay eyes on the tiny beige tents with their red flagpoles, billowing in the coastal breeze. The tiny specks of life passing between them: the shimmer of armour and the spark of swords like the dancing ripples of fish. The barricades erected at the base of the hillside, opening out on the narrow path that wound its way to the City of Arbash high above. A morning walk up that path, and they would be at their very gates. That this enemy, new and entirely unknown to them, were so close already. Waiting there in the cove, for the first strike of the kindling flame.

So close already, she whispered through her mind.

Hope, and a matter of time…

VIII

GREED

Three weeks later…

The weeks had passed by apprehensively since Dur'al joined the army in the west, and the house had seemed all but deserted for the silence that prevailed. As the family drifted around the rooms, hardly any words were exchanged between them, beyond the trivialities of asking how work was or who was cooking the evening meal. It seemed that every sentence – every sentiment, even – came with no life. Like haunted shadows, the family chose to shift through the gloom in utter silence, where not even the embrace of sleep offered them any solace.

As if nothing seemed right anymore.

After the conversation with the Hermit, My'ala had spent

most of her time in a numb daze: not as lost as the rest of the family seemed to be, but still unable to process any clear thought. She had gone to help her father at the workshop a number of times, only to find no customers would come, as no-one dared tend to their farms with an enemy just down the hillside. She had then gone to her mother's allotment to the north, hoping to pull their huge vegetables from the ground to make stew – only to find the allotments closed and boarded up, the plants taken under palace orders to be stored underground for a siege. So she had wandered aimlessly back to the house and disappeared into her room each day, sprawling out across her bed, hoping the next day would bring some respite.

Hoping on a whim, she found, as every tomorrow brought more of the same.

We are a people in despair, she mused, sat in the garden one day as the hummingbirds looped over her head. *We are lost, trying to reconcile our fear with our grief.* The hibiscus tree above, still as tall and proud as she remembered it being as a child, had finished its blossom for the year before the rains set in, and the floor around her lay littered with the tiny gaping mouths of its flowers. *All things come to pass.* She plucked one of the flowers from the ground, and found within its folds the tiny shape of a bee. Nestled in its final resting place with the hibiscus like a cocoon, My'ala placed it down on the dry earth again and covered it with soil.

The question is, when?

The young girl lifted to her feet and whispered a goodbye to her favourite tree, before turning and pacing the length of the garden to the open back door. Dinner would soon be ready, she knew: the sweet aroma of pickled vo'zan meat caught at her nostrils and tickled her tongue. She moved into the shadow of the house interior, finding within her a glimmer of joy at the thought of a warm cooked meal.

Growing starkly cold again, when she thought of the silence that would accompany it.

"How was work?" her mother asked at the table, spooning a mouthful of berries into her mouth to hide the shaking in her hands.

"It was quiet," her father replied bluntly, rolling his fingers together in slow circles. "No customers. The machines aren't selling at all at the moment... how was your work?"

"Tiring; very busy. Lots of paperwork."

"What are you working on at the moment?"

"Handling food supplies in the vaults. The numbers are... *concerning*, to say the least."

"Are people panicking?"

"Well there's a war going on, and we may be cooped up behind these walls for months. I mean, there are people fighting in the..." Her mother stopped herself, a quiver in her cheek. "It's no wonder people are afraid," she continued. "We're about to have our lives ripped up from beneath us, and there's seemingly nothing we can do..."

My'ala pushed the grapes around her plate absently with the end of her fork, both curious about her parents' conversation and actively trying to hide from it. Su'la, sat to the right of her, was doing much the same: like the grey clouds that first marked a coming storm, she hung her head low to her plate of half-dissected food with no appetite to give. When they had first sat down, My'ala had attempted to comfort her sister with a hand across the shoulder, noting her visible distress — but Su'la had flinched away, the mirage of tears in her eyes, and the young girl had left her sister alone for the remainder of the meal.

A sister who hardly says a word, My'ala thought. *A mother who busies herself with work to avoid reminders of her son. A father, even more quiet and insular than usual, making small talk for the sake of normalcy.*

And me in the middle, trying to make sense of it all.

"We should be grateful, I suppose, for the wonderful people who have organised the vaults to be used in the first place," her mother cooed softly. "Without their involvement, we would likely have no place to store anything, if worst came to worst."

"Perhaps," their father replied glumly.

Her mother frowned. "What is it?"

"I wouldn't call it grateful, to watch people act in their own self-interest..."

"What do you mean?"

"Well, they do it because they hope they can be first in line for their families when the rationing begins... that's all it is. Do your bit and survive a bit longer."

"Can't you understand that maybe people do this out of the goodness of their hearts? Because they care about something bigger than themselves?"

Her father held his hands up in mock-surrender. "No

matter the moral stance taken by any decision they make, the result is always the same. If it came down to it, they would sooner stampede the lot of us to keep their families alive for a few more days, than be '*just*' and '*fair*' about it…"

"You don't see the good in people," her mother said venomously.

Her father shook his head. "No, I see the *truth* in people."

"Truth has blinded you."

"Your belief in human goodwill has blinded *you*."

Her mother grit her teeth. "Well, it doesn't matter. We shouldn't talk of these things. They're not good for——"

"Why not?"

My'ala watched as her mother's head snapped round to her, followed shortly after by her father's despondent gaze. Even Su'la froze, lowering her fork to the table.

"Mi," her sister muttered, "please don't…"

"No," My'ala interrupted, "why shouldn't we talk about these things? They're the reality of our situation, are they not? An enemy approaches – our people are dying in the field. Why should these things be silenced?"

The table went deathly silent for some moments, where not even the whisper of the wind dared pass through. My'ala's heartbeat rattled in her ears; she thought she would be sick.

To her right, Su'la lowered her head and sighed, making to leave – to her left, she watched her mother open her mouth, venom on her tongue——

Until her father held both his arms out suddenly, stopping the two women in their tracks.

With a forlorn glare, the older sister acceded, adjusting

back into her chair with her hands clasped in her lap. Their mother, meanwhile, sealed her lips like a trapdoor, and gazed out into the sunlit garden with heavy eyes.

My'ala studied her father for a second in silence, the weight of the world passing between them in the fractious light, before he finally opened his mouth and spoke to her in almost a daze.

"We talk of the good of humankind," he began. "We talk of our loving kindness, our responsibility... our *magnality*. Our ability to manage and survive and prosper. Putting food on tables and money in pockets. And we talk about these things because they make us feel good about ourselves. Because we are, to our own eyes as mortal beings, very special in the world. Unique, if you would. And we have also decided, in our most arrogant ways, that that uniqueness also makes us... *without fault*. And that no matter what we do – no matter what abhorrent thing we exact – it's okay, because we're still *unique*."

"We make excuses," My'ala inferred, watching her father nod.

"For every merchant, there's a fraud; for every charitable giver, there is a thief; for every builder, there's a saboteur. For every leader, there is a despot. For every doting parent, there is a neglectful drunk next door. For every act of good in this city, there is one of equal cruelty." He scoffed. "You see, I never had a problem with Dur'al going out to fight the invaders in the cove. It never crossed my mind, the danger he would face going out there. He was just doing what he felt was right. And I let him..."

My'ala's mother made to interrupt, a pleading sorrow in

her eyes, but her father waved her away.

"But it wasn't his choice, in the end, that reduced me to the silent husk of a man I am now," he continued, a sneer gracing his face. "It was his reason for going. It was that he wanted to go... out of the duty and care for those *less fortunate* than him. Less *fortunate*? Dur'al, and dozens just like him... young, proud people marching down that hillside toward the cove... ready to butcher and slaughter these newcomers, and be butchered and slaughtered themselves. And why? Well, out of the *goodness of humankind,* of course. For those *less fortunate* than them. Because they were good people doing an honourable thing..." He shook his head. "Or so they were *told...*"

"That's enough," her mother barked.

"And your mother here, is a prime example of what I mean," he pressed on. "Your ma has a heart of purest silver, and everything she does, she does with the intention of supporting others. Because everyone deserves a chance — everyone deserves food, and shelter, and *hope*. And I couldn't be prouder of that..." He sighed. "But I just know... I just *know* that there are others who don't. It could be a council member who has a secret set of keys, ready to pack half the stores into carts and ship them off into the desert on the whim of finding something out there, leaving the rest of us to starve. Or collectors bringing in the harvest, keeping secret stashes in their houses to feed their families when the rationing starts. People acting in their own self-interest, as they always have. And that's the truth of it — it's terrible, but that's what it is." His hand buckled into a fist. "Because humankind may be *good* and *fair* and so *perfect* in its way of life… but that also neglects our single greatest flaw: we are not in fact guided by love, or care, or duty, or common cause. We never have been. We are guided by one thing, and one thing alone…"

He inhaled slowly.

"*Greed.*"

"Enough!" My'ala's mother bellowed, lifting from her seat with a scrape of stone. Opposite her, Su'la placed her head in her hands and started sobbing, face a welt of despair. "We *don't* need to hear this! We are in *despair,* over what's happening. The entire city is! Your son is out there risking his *life,* fighting for—"

"What?"

Her mother gulped; her father at the end of the table rose to his feet.

"What exactly is he fighting for?" he growled. "He isn't fighting for any of us, is he? We were distraught when he went, and rightly so. He isn't fighting for honour, either, because what honour is there in putting your life at risk to kill others?" He speared a finger out into the empty air. "What it is, is that he's gone out there, headstrong and hopeful, plagued by the arrogant decisions of hierarchy. Because people are greedy, and people are violent, and all that people know deep down inside, is *hate.*"

"You're hysterical." My'ala's mother shook her head. "People are not full of hate – they're full of blindness, just as *you* are. Business has made you shrewd and cynical – you can no longer see the sun for the clouds."

"I see a true reflection of what people are capable of. It's already claimed Dur'al… I only pray it doesn't claim anyone else here. We can't lose anymore…"

He stopped and glanced across the table to his two daughters then, for a moment – realising, for the first time, that both of them were nearing tears.

"And look what you're doing, saying these things," their mother exclaimed, all the strength gone from her voice. "They don't want to hear this. They don't want to hear about hate, and violence. Why would they—"

"We do want to hear it," My'ala said defiantly, steeling herself and making to stand. And as she did so, Su'la lifted her head from her hands, and – for the first time in weeks – My'ala saw a smile cross her sister's face.

And her heart began to sing.

"We deserve to hear these things," she continued. "We should not have reality hidden from us anymore. I am over sixteen-rain's old – Su'la is over twenty. I will not cower from the nature of our kind – I will not cower from the hate and greed we can cause. And I will not shy away from saying that both of you are wrong."

A look of shock passed between her parents, which in the end only bolstered her more.

"People are neither inherently good nor bad. The choices we make, likewise, are not as clear as day and night can be. There comes clouds, and there comes rain. Things are not always as they seem." She nodded. "Dur'al did what he believed in, by joining the army, even if you can't see it. Ma, you serve this city on the council, and provide for people – Da, you command your business with your family in mind, no matter the cost. Su'la studies human nature, so she can better understand how we see the world – and maybe, one day, she can help us understand it for the better. For all of us. Because we are neither right nor wrong in these choices – and morality is as the river runs. Good people do bad things; bad people do good things. Humankind, by that estimation, is neither greedy and hateful, nor loving and kind. We exhibit all of both... and should hide from none."

My'ala placed her hands on the table, and looked between all three of them.

"So remember, in all this, that we are a family. That we all love, and care, and loathe, and trust, and hate. And that these feelings we have, and beliefs we hold... we should never let them come between us. Because this is the time to come together, and put those differences aside. Because forgiveness, is the first step of hope... and with hope, we can achieve anything..."

Her words echoed out across the table like the undulating waves of the sea – and, for a moment, her parents stood speechless, gazing wide-eyed at their youngest daughter in almost disbelief. Trying to make sense of her: this sweet, quiet girl who loved hummingbirds and wrote poems and ate gojan fruits like grapes. The girl they had watched grow up for sixteen rain's past, always wanting the best and expecting nothing in return.

A girl who had just answered the wrongs of the world before their very eyes.

"We need each other," the young girl said, finding her strength and her smile. "Let's not lose sight of that..."

Like the trickles that marked the coming rain, My'ala watched as her sister beamed at her, the salt-stained marks under her eyes melting away like butter. Watched as her parents — arguing moments before then — looked to each other with forgiving eyes and wrapped their arms tightly. Watched as the hummingbirds alighted in the garden to her right: tiny gold coins dancing in the heat like the twinkling dots of stars.

As the glow of mid-afternoon sun swept through the windows across the table, and cast the room in ember shades of yellow and rust, My'ala felt her own heart begin to settle too. The shadows across the ceiling dissipated; the cold air around her flushed with a newfound warmth; the ghosts of her family seemed to drift from the house — replaced instead by the lights of human souls, drawing closer to orbit once again.

The young girl watched it all unfold around her, almost like watching a wound heal, and gave a sigh of relief to the aching knots of her hearts.

Perhaps things will be okay, My'ala thought with hope in her eye.

Perhaps this is not the end…

And then a knock sounded at their door, drawing their attention as boots navigated through the house toward them, echoing louder and louder, until a figure appeared in the doorway with steel-capped boots and a fine suit of armour.

My'ala's eyes lit up.

But it was not Dur'al who stood before them.

"Is this the house of Dur'al Busskar?" the officer said plainly, his steely grey eyes dark and forlorn.

"It is?" their father replied.

"Well, sir… we have some information about your son."

My'ala's heart seemed to stop.

No—

"We regret to inform you that, during the attacks this morning on the road up to the city, your son was engaged in the fighting, and was hit with an arrow through the neck." A heavy sigh. "He was... confirmed dead at the scene, and buried with the rest of his regiment on the hillside outside the city walls..." The officer lowered his eyes. "We are incredibly sorry for your loss."

No...

My'ala, stood at the end of the table in the sobering light, found she couldn't move. Found that she could not breathe, nor think, nor even comprehend the words that had left the officer's mouth. Her heart seemed to stall as she became suddenly short of breath. That the air became thin around her, filtering through her teeth like a dripping faucet. Hands trembling.

He's dead? she mouthed, lost from reality.

I can't... this can't be—

A wail, cracking the dead silence spread between them. My'ala looked over as her mother collapsed, legs failing her, emotions exploding across the room like aching thunder...

Her father reeled, holding her mother aloft, sucking air through his lips in tiny bursts as an unrelenting horror bit across his face...

Su'la, sat welded to her seat alongside them, placed her hands across her mouth and screamed...

And the healing she had seen was immediately shattered, taken by the horns of grief.

This can't be happening. She leant heavily against the table, a torrent rising through her chest. *This can't be... what happened to us? Was duty not supposed to protect him, when he went off to risk his life? What happened to the fearless pride? To the joy of life and service?*

Are we to blame? She inhaled at length, her lungs shivering. *Have we done this? Did we not love enough? Did we not fight enough when he decided the army was the only way? Should we have done more?*

Should I have done more to save him?

My'ala retched, nausea ripping through her body.

This is all so wrong. This shouldn't be happening. Purpose, duty; love and care; passion; ruthlessness... what's the point?

The grief within her swelled into numbness. Numbness, in turn, grew into anger.

There is no meaning of life. There is no purpose to this world. We are futile creatures, clutching at our own survival. No matter how much love you give, or passion you have, or what the cost is...

It doesn't mean anything, in the end.

My'ala lifted her gaze to her grieving family. Scanned the emptiness in the air. Crossed to the officer stood morbidly to one side, delaying the courage to console them, rubbing his fingers together with an awkward shuffle of his feet.

Saw the light of the front door down the hallway just beyond.

My'ala grit her teeth, open palms curling to tight fists. *I know who has to answer for this,* she thought bitterly. *I know who needs to hear that my brother is dead.*

Without a word of grief or consultation, My'ala slipped from the table and pushed past the officer, moving toward the open door like a surging rapid.

The hate in her heart longing to scream.

IX

THE ABYSS

The sky was the colour of rusted gold, as the sun lowered its head and brought the coming darkness. With light spilling out down the valley below, the groves of olives and clementines lay still. They had been stripped of their cargo over the previous nights like a ship run aground, the fruits of their labour carted off to the city to be boxed and secured in the vaults. All across the valley, deep tracks and horse hooves wound their way up to the walls of Arbash, truncating the earth like freshly tilled soil as far as the eye could see. And those carts had been the last of those to venture outside of the city walls: because when dusk fell, and night took hold, the gates would be sealed shut. None would leave and none would enter. All that would remain beyond the walls would be the circling shapes of vultures scouring the distant cliffs.

And the emboldened enemy snaking their way up the hillside to the west, with boots marching and swords glinting, hungry for the taste of blood.

Why is this happening? My'ala thought, traipsing across the dry earth in disbelief, wiping the last tears from her eyes. *What have we done to deserve this? Have we failed the God-King? Have we not been true to ourselves? Perhaps father was right: perhaps we are greed-driven, hating creatures. Perhaps that is all there is to us.*

Perhaps this is the cost of it.

She looked up the small incline to the Prophet's Tree, scowling at its wide, ancient boughs. At the heresy it represented, and all the wrongs of the world it dismissed. How wrong she felt, having put her trust in it.

And almost instinctively, the jade leaves seemed to bristle as she approached, and the heavy branches of the upper reaches recoiled at her burgeoning anger.

There is no meaning of life, she scolded. *There is no shared goal between all people. How can there be? How can there be unity among us and our beliefs, when humankind can be so cruel? People have died... my own brother, taken from me... because of what? Purpose? Duty?* She ground her teeth, biting back tears. *It doesn't mean anything anymore. It doesn't matter. There is no point. We live and we survive, and we clasp to whatever we can to do so. Because humanity is not only beautiful and greedy.*

It is also lost.

Cresting the rise, she found Artemis was already stood awaiting her, his hands clasped in front of him. He stood solemnly, with much of his face shrouded by the hood of his robe, as My'ala marched up to him and stopped a few feet away, fists clenched and jaw tight.

"It's all a *lie*," she spat, fiery in the orange glow of the sun. "It's all *wrong*."

"What is a lie, my dear?" Artemis asked, equal parts concerned and apprehensive.

"Everything we've talked about, all of it. *Lies*."

"Why? What has happened?"

"Dur'al is dead, Artemis!" she bellowed, letting the tears fall from her cheeks like tiny, salt-bitten streams. "My brother is *dead*... he went to fight, for *duty*, and now he's dead!"

A glint of his eyes shimmered in the dark of his hood. "My'ala, I... I'm so sorry..."

"I should've done more. I should've done more for him!" Her nails dug into her palms. "It's all a lie, this meaning of life. There is no point, or purpose to it. I let my brother go, because I believed he was doing what gave him *purpose*. I let him go, because I believed duty would *protect* him. And now he's *dead*... now he's dead, and I didn't so much as raise my voice against it. Because I *let him go*."

"My'ala, he... he did what he felt was right—"

"What good is doing what's right if you end up dead!"

My'ala sensed her legs start to give way, the light spinning behind her eyes. She lowered herself to the floor steadily with a flush of dust, straddling sideways in pain. With her hands held against her face, she finally let go of the knot of emotion that had wound itself so tightly around her heart. The broken twine of grief that ate away at her soul. Tears fell, billowing from her in streams, and the world seemed to darken all of a sudden – before she realised the Hermit had approached, his robes pooling at his feet as he crouched down to her level.

"I can't believe I let him go," she muttered. "I can't believe it…"

"It wasn't your fault," he replied. "You let him do what he felt was right."

"But now he's dead."

"He knew the risks of his actions…"

My'ala shook her head. "It doesn't make it any easier on us, though, now that we face the consequences."

"I'm not saying it does: I'm incredibly sorry for the pain this has caused you, and what you have lost. I'm so sorry."

"What's the point, Artemis?" She lifted her hands and shrugged. "What's the point in looking up to the stars, trying to find the meaning of life, when life itself can be so meaningless? When it can be so cruel and hurtful? What do you see there? Am I missing something?"

My'ala moved her hands away from her face, and looked deep into the starlit wells of the Hermit's eyes, seeing there a thousand twinkling figments scattered across a black-blue sky. She saw infinite possibility, reflected in the infinite void that seemed almost to consume her soul. She saw every ounce of humanity – all its triumphs and malcontents strewn into one – and couldn't make sense of any of it.

And it was only then, that she realised the Hermit was crying.

"You're weeping…" she said absently, from shock more than anything else.

Artemis closed his eyes for a heartbeat, and looked out on

the sinking sun.

"I am, yes," he mused softly.

"Why?"

He purses his lips. "I think it's about time I told you a story, My'ala: the story of how I ended up here, with the night sky in my eyes… many, many moons ago…"

The young girl relaxed her shoulders suddenly, the tidal storm in her chest quelling for a moment.

"I used to have a family, like yours," the Hermit began. "I had a wife, and a beautiful young boy. We lived out in the desert, many leagues from here, in a small stone house beside a huge oasis. We grew vegetables from the rich soil around it, and hunted the animals who drank from it for food. Me and my boy would scale palm trees taller than cliff-faces and dangle from the top like hanging fruit, looking out over the rolling dunes every morning as the sun began to emerge. I always remembered it being a good life… it was melodic and purposeful. I tended to the crops, scavenged for food, and kept the house up together for my family. And I found a sort of *meaning*, in those idle tasks: that to be content and dutiful in the day-to-day of one's life, was to find a peace within yourself unlike any other. And, tending to the crops around the soft-sand edges of that oasis… I thought that would be my life forevermore…"

The Hermit's mouth became a harsh line as he adjusted his robes.

"Then, one day, a sandstorm swept in. Nothing unusual, of course, given where we lived… but this one was far worse than any we'd seen before. We treated it as normal and sheltered in the house for some time, living off our food reserves that we kept stored under the beds to keep cool, singing sweet songs to my boy to get him to sleep through the howling winds." He struggled to swallow. "But what we thought was a sandstorm that would only last a few turns of the sun, became a maelstrom lasting three whole days, and continued on with no sign of stopping. Our food supplies ran out almost immediately; by the third night, my boy was deathly pale from lack of water, and my wife couldn't stop crying. I feared for their survival, every day that passed – I… I knew something had to be done. So I went out into the storm on the fourth day, with nothing more than a satchel and a stick to hold me in place, to see what I could find by the water's edge. And out of fear… out of fear for my life, my boy… my *dear* boy opened the door behind me to call out to me, and a gust of the storm tore through the house." A single tear rolled down his cheek. "All I heard was the snap of palm wood and the grinding of old stone, and I knew what had happened. It only took the scream of my wife, suddenly and fatally cut short, to know my life was all but over."

My'ala blinked slowly, the shock coiling up her spine as she absorbed the Hermit's story. "I… I'm so sorry…"

"I lay in the rubble of my home for what felt like an eternity, weeping softly as the storm tore across my body, ripping across my skin… and I really thought I would die that day," he said morbidly, shadows across his skin. "And then, for whatever reason, the storm suddenly stopped. The sky cleared; the great blue unravelled overhead like dyed cloth. And in my rags, starving and parched, I pulled myself up from what remained of my house and screamed to the gods for what they had done to me, not knowing who else to blame…"

"But there was no one to blame," the young girl remarked. "It was nature that claimed them."

"We will always blame ourselves, if there are no others. It's how we manage our grief as people, and I did as any other would. But then I looked outward – taking in the world, rather than letting it swallow me – and found something there. I looked out on the broken stone and the ruined crops and the oasis that was now little more than a well… and I saw that I was not alone. That, in its own way, the world around me was grieving too. That we had suffered together; that we had survived together. And at that moment, there came a thought, experiencing the shared grief that I was." He lifted a finger. "That there is still meaning in the world after all, and there is always something more…"

My'ala exhaled, and sat surprised at the relief she felt. "What did you do?" she asked.

"I gathered what I could." He nodded. "And with a satchel and a stick, I started walking out into the desert, hoping to find something there. I had no idea what, nor what direction I was going in. I could not tell you how far I walked, or for how many nights. All I knew, was that there was something more out there." Something resembling a smile crossed his face. "And, somehow, I ended up here… and I found my purpose again."

He lifted a hand and placed it on her shoulder, squeezing tightly, gazing into My'ala's eyes with the deepness of stars.

"I cannot undo what has been done, and there are no words I can say that will properly express how deeply sorry I am for your loss," Artemis said softly. "But, know that this is not the end. That all is not lost. It is from the deepest point of a well, that the light will shine strongest above. It is there, in the lowest depths of our mind and soul, that we find our true purpose, and find meaning in this cruel and fickle life. So do not give up, My'ala… do not give in. There is so much to treasure in this world, even if it seems unthinkable now. And I know it, because *I've seen it.* So please keep fighting, and keep asking the questions you always have. And when you go home this evening, and look down the streets of your great city, see that you are not alone — that in these darkest moments, when all seems lost, all anyone needs is a spark…"

He smiled, warm and beautiful like a crescent moon.

"All they need, is a *tiny glimmer of hope.*"

My'ala let the sensations rise and fall in her chest like a sparkling stream, flowing over and through her body as the Hermit's words took hold. An uncertainty slowly claimed her, numb and fragile. Like a vulture on the verge of its nest, she felt close to taking off, an airiness to her body consuming all things. And a thought gravitated to the forefront of her mind, like the glistening strike of a prophet's star, and the Sentinel tree high above leaned over her in a natural embrace.

Dur'al is gone, but he would not want us to lose ourselves too, she thought, thinking of his face and his smile. *With hundreds of others at risk from the same enemy that claimed him… he would want only one thing. He would want their safety —* our *safety. He would want us to go on and find purpose again in our lives and the world around us. He'd want us to prevail.*

And believe.

My'ala lifted her hands to the arm resting on her shoulder, and clasped the Hermit's hand in her own.

"Thank you, Artemis, and… and I'm sorry," My'ala stuttered. "The pain I feel is not yours, and should not be made yours."

"No need to apologise, my dear," the Hermit replied. "Our pain is shared, always – for that way, it becomes smaller, not bigger. I shall take whatever pain you have, if it means a lighter load on your shoulders. Always."

She smiled, fresh tears in her eyes. "Thank you."

He squeezed her hand and braced her forearm, making to stand and hoist her to her feet.

"Now you best get back to the city… I expect they will be closing the gates soon. You need to be with your family and be safe."

"But what about you?" My'ala exclaimed. "What will you do?"

"You need have no fear for me, my dear." He smiled. "I have seen the vastness of night and the most beautiful seas this desert has ever known… I will be fine, I assure you. Now go, please, and be safe My'ala. Your family need you." A pause. "And I think you'll find, in the end, that your people may need you too."

My'ala found her words betray her, caught on the end of her tongue – and as she made to finally speak, the Hermit was shooing her off, back down the hillside and off towards the walls of Arbash.

In the red glow of approaching dusk, her eyes did not leave the painted robes and starlit eyes of the old man atop the hill. She watched his presence grow slowly smaller, under the pearlescent shape of the Prophet's Tree, wondering all the while what would come next.

And if that was the last time she would ever see him.

X

GRIEF

She stepped through the gates of Arbash in the red glow of dusk, and saw all around her that the world was weeping.

The guards on the other side hurried her through the gap before they were sealed shut again: tired, quivering hands pulling the massive iron bar across to seal off the outside world. Their faces were white as cloth sheets, hollowed eyes like corpses. They flinched at every sound, every turn of the wind as it passed. Those along the walls seemed to cower in the alcoves of the gatehouse, peering up into the bleeding sky as if it were about to collapse above them.

My'ala shivered at the sight of them, fearful of the desperation in their eyes. She turned and started walking down the long street ahead as it curved slowly west into the city beyond, the echo of her footsteps impeccably loud in the eerie quiet of night.

Eyes on stilts, the young girl scanned the squat homes around her and saw everywhere the signs of human grief. Peering through a window, a man sat at his desk, hands on his head in disbelief, sprawls of his memoirs etched across the reed-paper before him that no-one would ever read. Looking just ahead, a mother sat in a doorway to a tavern with a baby nestled in her arms, sobbed and muttered quiet prayers to it, wishing everything to be okay. Above, the sounds of screaming suddenly blared out from an upstairs window, as a family battled over whether to cut their losses and run or face the enemy tide that was sure to come.

My'ala walked among them, passing house after house, and thought of the terror in their hearts. Of how little hope there was left among the people of Arbash, cowering behind the walls of the greatest kingdom the world had ever known.

Or so they had assumed.

Although now perhaps not.

How wrong we were, to think we were the only ones, she mused. *In the vastness of this land, in this world… we thought all this time that we were the only civilisation to ever exist. How foolish we were, to even entertain it.*

How horrifying reality has become.

Stopping for a moment, the young girl was drawn to the sound of muttered voices, and turned to find the warm orange glow of an open prayer house next to her. The room, although being no bigger than a living space, was packed to each corner with people prostrating. And at the far end, clutching a lectern, an ancient-looking woman with straggled grey hair and dour eyes expressed her sympathies to the God-King in their time of need. In a hushed voice, she spoke of a need for guidance, and that a new path forward had to reveal itself if their people were to survive. It was almost a plea, intermittently affirmed by the unified whisper of the gathered crowd, pronouncing their service to the God-King in hope of his mercy.

In times of desperate need, people turn to the unknown for answers, My'ala thought, carrying on down the street. *Some rally to their families, hoping the end is quick when it comes. Others plan for escape, to survive in whatever manner they can. A few may arm themselves, barricading doors and hiding possessions in the hopes the enemy are impressed and let them live.* She sighed.

And some wander the streets as night descends, wondering what answers lie in the stars.

At the thought, she looked up with wandering eyes as the shimmering dots appeared in the sky, the night descending like a blanket to set a baby softly to sleep. She saw tiny specks no bigger than grains of sand, alongside other ones that were almost as big as grapes — she saw some that shot across the sky like the arc of a catapult, disappearing into the ether just as quickly as they had arrived. Flecks of paint across a black-blue canvas, My'ala marvelled at the sheer size of the night above, and grew dizzy trying to count just how stars may have been up there in the vastness of nothing beyond.

What does Artemis see up there? she pondered, eyes darting between each cluster of life. *There is so much up there... so many lights and shapes and colours. Some move and some pulse. No night sky is ever like the last, or the first, or the next. Forever chang-*

ing, right above our heads.

And many of us don't even realise.

She inhaled through her nose in a great stream, and exhaled through pursed lips like a blacksmith's hearth.

Although maybe that's the point: like prayers to the God-King, maybe we accept that the night sky is an unknown too. A vast, infinitely-possible thing that we can never comprehend, but want to try to nonetheless. Because it isn't fear that drives us into the unknown of the world at all. It's curiosity.

It's hope.

My'ala turned suddenly, looking off to the eastern walls – knowing, beyond their interlocking stones, that a massive desert stretched off to the horizon just the other side of it. A vast unknown, as great as the night-sky could ever be, that had been fearfully ignored for generations as a nothingness like no other.

But she thought back, then, to the story Artemis had told her on the hillside: of oases, and palm trees, and life and survival. Of *purpose,* even more so.

Finding purpose in the everyday. She nodded her head. *That there is always something more. Because at our lowest ebb, the light we seek is not one of fear or desperation.*

It is a belief, and a hope, that the unknown will answer us.

And all we have to do, is start walking...

"What are you doing?"

She was drawn back to reality, startled by the presence of a small boy at her side, dressed in rags with a small bowl in his hand. A street urchin, she assumed: one of the city's abandoned lot.

You've seen hard times like these all before, ay?

"I'm just heading home," she replied quietly.

"Have you seen what's happening outside the walls?" he replied, almost surprised she had answered him. "There are torches and marching people with swords. Everyone is hiding from them… everyone is saying that we're doomed."

A pang of sadness in her heart. "People are afraid. It's only natural."

"Are we doomed, miss?" he asked, the big hazel rounds of his eyes shimmering up toward her. "Do you think we are doomed?"

My'ala, hardly double the boy's age, crouched down to draw level with him and smiled. "I don't believe we are, no… I don't think we're doomed."

"Why is that?"

Like the welcome sight of home, she looked up to the stars. "Because whatever comes next, is always an unknown. We do not know what tomorrow, or the next day, or the next rainy season shall bring. And what we face outside our walls… well, it's just another uncertainty, no different than the million we face every day just be living." She nodded. "It is fear that tells us to give up – fear that tells us we are doomed. That there is no answer, nor way out. And if we accept that, and allow it to rot the good inside us, then that is all we'll ever know. But it doesn't have to be that way: we face the unknown with every action we take. The unknown, in a weird way, is so natural to us. And in times like these, when the enemy rally their swords and we cannot, we must find it within us to rally our hearts instead, and find a way. And that's the beautiful thing about the unknown: it can be whatever you want it to be. The spark that lights the fire, and saves us all, is simple."

She met his eyes.

"It's *hope*."

The boy nodded, an astonished joy in his complexion. "But… but who will be that hope?"

My'ala blinked slowly, aware of the boys words – suddenly becoming aware of everything, all at once. Of the city around her; the grief at the loss of her brother; the despair and fear of what was to come; the conversation with the Hermit on the hillside. Love. Care. Ruthlessness. Duty. Grief. Pain. Hope. That there was always something more – always another path ahead.

And someone must voice it.

She lifted to a stand, looking off down the street towards her house – knowing the council would rally tomorrow, her mother amongst them, and the city would come to hear their words declaring all hope was lost. It was an inflection point, like the first spot of rain to bring the coming storm. It was a single moment, where someone could change the fate of the kingdom.

A single moment, where she could decide what the unknown would become.

"Someone will show them that there is still hope," My'ala told the boy, eyes like tiny fires. "Someone will show them what the meaning of life really is, and how there's always another way." She drew the words from deep within her soul, a realisation catching at the tip of her tongue. Inhaling, exhaling, the swell of the moon high above.

Knowing the someone she spoke of, was her.

XI

HOPE

The following day…

As the midday sun crested the sky overhead, illumi-
nating the squat buildings and high palisade walls
with an almost marbled brightness, the citizenry of
Arbash amassed in the city's main plaza with expectant eyes,
awaiting their fates at the hands of the council. Trepidation
filled the air, as people lined the balconies and perched along
flat rooftops to survey the huge crowd beneath them. Hundreds upon hundreds of people jostled together on the hot
stone slabs, muttering faithlessly to each other, looking
ahead to the raised platform and the domed rotunda of the
God-Elect's Palace.

It was a marvel to see, in the dazzling light of high-sun: a
single structure of immense proportions, lined with carved

statues and pillars, huge struts at each corner where billowing flags were butchered by a sea wind. The dome that made up the majority of the roof was arranged in segments, bound by what many believed to be solid gold, so as to look like rich veins flowing between the stonework. It was said, in ancient legend, that the flag-stone of the God-Elect's Palace was the founding stone of the entire city, placed by the hands of the Prophets themselves many millennia ago. And that if one looked closely over the brow of the raised platform, they could still see the cracked, yellowed stone of that first block wedged against the base of the doorway. How it stood as a testament of times gone past — of a hundred generations come and gone.

A sign of just what was at stake, and what was about to unfold.

"Are you sure about this?" My'ala's mother asked, placing a hand on her daughter's shoulder. They stood adjacent to the raised platform, under a hastily-erected canopy to shield them from the worst of the sun's rays. Sweat still reamed down their backs, however, as the warm air grew even heavier.

"I promise, ma," My'ala replied, wiping her brow clear, aware of the wandering eyes of the other members of the council just behind. Many of them wore a look of disdain like a rash whenever she caught their gaze.

Clearly they don't think I have anything of value to say, the young girl thought with a sneer. *That I'm too young — what could someone like me possibly know?*

"I'm really putting my neck out for you to do this, Mi." Her mother's tired, sleepless eyes met her own. "With everything that's happened, I… I don't really know what to do anymore. I don't know what is right or wrong… everything conventional that we've ever known, is gone."

"I know, ma… and I'm here to correct that. I believe I can show them another way forward. A way that doesn't mean condemning us to a merciless end."

"Okay. But you won't have long, Mi… once the God-Elect has given their report, you have a short time to speak before the other council members want to give their verdict." She squeezed her shoulder. "So, whatever it is that you have to say… please make it work."

"I will, ma, I promise."

A pause for a moment. "Your da and Su'la are very proud of you, I hope you know that," her mother said softly, a half-beaten smile gracing her face. "We all are."

My'ala returned the smile. "Thank you, ma."

"It seems we all, as a family, wanted to do our bit to be purposeful and do good in this life. All in our own different ways. And now, as things often seem to go… this may well be yours."

"I hope so." She nodded. "I've learned a lot, over the years, about what kind of people we should be, and what we should do in our times of need. Of what to do, when it looks like we've reached the end of the road. I just hope what I say here can reassure people of that, and that they listen."

"People will always listen, Mi… especially when it seems like there's no way out. I'm just worried they won't see things the way you do. I'm worried they've condemned themselves before the decision has even been made."

My'ala drew in a long breath at her mother's words.

You and me both…

They were drawn suddenly to the sounds of trumpets, bellowing out from the high balconies of the palace behind. My'ala turned from her mother, and her gaze was drawn to the golden double-doors as the entranceway pulled gently open. From within, palace guards in armoured plates emerged from the shadows, bearing a crimson-red canopy between them on long poles. And beneath its shaded cover, an austere figure with striking blonde hair and blood-red robes strode out toward the platform, hands clasped before them as if in prayer.

The God-Elect, My'ala thought, a tenseness rising in her chest. *The elected representative of Arbash, ordained by God-King the Creator. I've never seen him in the flesh before.*

The canopy reached the edge of the platform and stopped suddenly, and My'ala watched as the God-Elect pulled his hair back and stepped out into the blazing sun.

With a shimmer like lightning, lines of silver thread exploded across his robes, like a thousand shooting stars dicing between each other. He seemed to glisten miraculously before them, as the crowd below bowed their heads and raised hands to their chests in admiration.

How incredible.

"Citizens of Arbash!" the God-Elect boomed, raising his hands, projecting his voice far and wide. "We find ourselves in desperate times, lost and without direction, as an enemy set up camp outside our walls and ready their engines of war. Never before, in our known history, has Arbash been assailed by another people. Never before has another wished ill upon us, and rallied their weapons against us. And now, in these uncertain times, we face an enemy that we neither know of nor understand, and our very lives are under threat because of them. The offensive was lost" – the God-Elect lowered his gaze – "and many of you lost friends and family in the fighting. For that I can only offer my sympathies, and mourn their sacrifice. But where the offensive failed, we must now place our faith in the *defensive*. That, I believe, is where this fight shall be won: not in the strike of our blades, but in the strength of our hearts to go on."

The God-Elect gestured over to the council alongside him, and My'ala thought she caught the flash of his pale-grey eyes.

"As is customary among our traditions," he continued, "the chosen council of Arbash shall now express to you their decision about our way forward in this difficult time. So, lend your ears to them, and take stead in their wisdom. Let us stand together, and find our strength in their words."

The God-Elect took several steps backward, moving beneath the crimson canopy alongside his guards, opening the stage for the council to speak.

For me to speak, My'ala gulped.

The young girl looked back fearfully, dismissing the other council members who sneered her way, and found the glossy eyes of her mother staring back at her.

Everything drew silent and still suddenly. Life ceased to be. The world and all its malcontents seemed, for at least a while, pointless. There was just an empty space, shared innately between them, stretching out into the forever. A space where, despite the grief racking her heart, My'ala's mother found it in her to smile, blushed and beautiful, and whispered a few tiny words that made the young girl's soul alight.

"*You can do it, Mi.*"

And suddenly My'ala found herself turning, brought back to reality, moving onto the raised platform in long strides. Stopping at the centre – where moments before the God-Elect had stood – and lifting her arm to the sun blaring high in the sky overhead. Aware of the voices below: the inquiring mutters of the crowd. Inhaling deeply through the vacuum of her chest.

Now or never, she thought, fingers trembling at her sides. *The fate of the kingdom, resting in my hands…*

"People of Arbash!" she said aloud, only just audible above the chatter of those below her. "I am here with a message for you! And I am here with a plea, also, to those in power. Although I am not a member of the council myself, and do not hold the stately credentials of those beside me… I wish only for a few moments of your time to hear what I have to say!"

Her heart tensed, as the eager faces spread across the plaza before her turned into frowns and muted glares. Words passed between them – confusion, mostly, but also distrust. My'ala flinched at the sound of grating metal behind her, as the wary palace guards drew closer around the God-Elect, fearing the worst.

Keep it together Mi, she told herself, rolling her tongue across her teeth. *They need to hear this.*

Their lives may depend on it.

"We are a city that lives in fear of what tomorrow brings," she began, almost as a shout. "We are a people who have prospered in our way of life for generations. Ancestors of the great Prophets, who raised this city with their bare hands. We have tilled the soil and built our palaces, and we have made this place our home. We are proud of who we are – and as we should be! Behold, around us, the fruits of our labour: such a beautiful city is Arbash!"

With a sudden flourish of life, the mutterings in the crowd before her stopped. Heads started to turn, and approving nods passed among them like the bobbing heads of birds.

Perhaps she *did* have something to say…

"And now, as we stand here, that way of life is under threat," My'ala continued. "Because an enemy, the likes of which we have never seen before, camp just outside our western gates. With steel and venom, they have come to our shores. And many of those closest to us – my… my brother included – have died by their hand…"

She bit down the emotion that swelled, channelling it through her words.

"We are a city that grieves, and fears the worst in what comes next. Because we do not know what happens, now that they have come… we do not know what will become of our city, and our people, and our ways of life. We are preparing for a siege, as it stands: preparing to man our walls and ration our food; to board our houses and outstay our new enemy, hoping they turn tail and go back whence they came. We hope, therefore, for preservation. We hope to keep our way of life, and live on unchanged… even as battering rams rip through our gates, and fires ravish our farmlands. We will carry on as if nothing is wrong, even while the enemy marches down our streets…"

A number of the crowd before her jostled on the spot —
My'ala sensed commotion at her side, as the other council
members protested her words. She pursed her lips.

They need to hear it.

"But I know you are no fools!" she pronounced. "I see that
you already know this. We have an enemy at our gates, that
can be resupplied by the sea: reinforcements, armour,
weapons, whatever you can think of. All shipped in and
hauled up the hill in half a day. But still we continue on with
preparations for a siege — to weather the storm that comes
— expecting them to one day just give up and leave us. But
you know, as well as I do, just how persevering humankind
can be. And how ruthless they can become, when someone
else claims what they want…"

Her father's voice echoed through her mind, and she
sighed.

"So, I can see no other way that this ends. The enemy shall
come for us. They will batter our walls, tear our gates down,
and march through our streets. They will drag us out of our
homes, and from there who knows what they will do. Our
fate almost seems to be decided — and because of that, we
may have already lost. To endure a siege, is to delay what
may become the inevitable. And we are, all of us, risking
our lives in doing so." She paused. "Unless, that is, we're
willing to go another way…"

A commotion suddenly sounded at her side, and My'ala
turned to find a scene of anarchy unfolding as her mother
and a few other council members held their colleagues at
bay. Between her mother's outstretched arms, My'ala saw
those others snarl and cry her way, calling her a heretic and

a traitor; cruel and dismissing. She heard the glide of metal swords leaving their sheaths at her back, as the palace guards readied to engage. And before her, a crowd who stood fearfully, anticipating what came next, awaiting My'ala's words.

The young girl bit her tongue. *It's either this, or the end,* she thought, clenching her fists.

And I'm not going down without fighting for it.

"Know that you are not alone, in the fear you have for your future!" she bellowed, silencing the rabble that had developed at her side in an instant. "Know that you are not alone in your grief, and your unease, and your despair. And know, too, that this is not the only way." She lifted her hand out west toward the sea. "What we face, is an unknown. A brute uncertainty that we cannot predict. And we fear the unknown, by its very nature. Because our way of life is certain... and the unknown, is most certainly not."

There were several scattered nods among the crowd at her feet.

"But why should we fear it? Why should we fear the unknown? We face it every day: every decision we make, different to the last, is uncertain. And yet we face it, almost as easily as drawing breath. We challenge that which challenges us. And why should this be no different? Why consign ourselves to fate, trying to salvage whatever remnant of our way of life we can? Because will it be worth it, honestly, to do so? What life is there to live, if we just cling to the past?"

My'ala puffed her chest out, sensing the heat radiate across her skin. She lifted an arm to the east, toward the desert.

"I know of someone – a wise man, with the night sky in his eyes – who told me something yesterday. He told me that, at our lowest point, the light we seek shines brightest. That there is always something more... that there is always another path. He lived out in the desert once before, and one day his home was destroyed in a sandstorm; his family, buried under the rubble; his crops outside, torn to shreds as the oasis became little more than a puddle. And he thought, as we do now, that he had lost everything – that there was nothing more in this life to give. But it was also at that time, looking on what remained of his life, that he realised he had only lost what he *knew*. And that the world, unchanging and evermore, still pressed on as it always had." She offered her hands out to them. "So, we must ask ourselves, here and now, whether we are willing to find that path ahead. If we are strong enough to challenge the uncertainty that rises against us. Because even though our house still stands, and our crops still grow and our loved ones still surround us, it only takes a storm to wipe that all away. And now the storm is upon us, outside our walls, with steel and swords and hate. And if we don't choose this new path, and face the unknown, then we may never get that chance again..."

"What are you suggesting we do?" someone in the crowd beneath her shouted, to the mumbled agreement of those around them.

"I say we load the food supplies onto carts," she proclaimed. "We gather our possessions, whatever we can carry. We seal the vaults and open the eastern gates." She paused. "We put our faith in the desert, and head out onto the sands, and face the unknown in search of our purpose..."

As she finished, gasps ruptured across the crowd before her. People looked to each other in disbelief. One of the council members beside her screeched.

"What choice do we have!" My'ala cried out. "We either head into the desert, or hand ourselves over to the mercy of the enemy!" She paused, placing a hand on her heart. "We must do this, because we forget who we are. *What* we are. The city of Arbash may be the greatest city the world has ever known… but in the end, it is still just a city. A city as any other. Because we are not defined by the stone beneath out feet – we are *defined,* by the unity we have as people, and the strength we hold in our hearts. For this city is little more than a familiarity. And where we belong, is not a place: it is *within us.*" She thumped a fist against her chest. "So let go of your fears! Challenge the unknown: we are nothing, if not for our power to persevere. We will live on; we will find another way. So gather your possessions. Rally your friends. Find hope within yourselves. Prepare to face the desert, and the unknown that will follow—"

Someone grappled her arm suddenly, and My'ala stumbled backwards. Almost falling; collapsing into someone's outstretched arms to save her. She looked up into the bright allure of the sun, dazed and beyond reality – finding one of the elder council stood where she had been moments ago, waving a fist angrily while addressing the crowd.

"The council has already decided!" the old woman screeched. "The decision has been made! Dismiss the words of this *traitor* as little more than heresy! We have decided – we shall weather the siege!"

She turned to My'ala with a growl.

"You have defied us!" the old woman charged. "You have defied us, and betrayed your people, and you are deserving of such harsh punishment beyond your… your…"

Like the changing tides of the aquamarine sea, the council member's face dropped. Her words failed to manifest. The entire crowd behind her seemed to withdraw in shock.

My'ala, only just aware of what was going on, blinked slowly. Her head was heavy, and the sun overhead was unrelenting bright. And it took several moments, far more than normal, before she realised that she was not fully standing, but rather leaning on something. So she looked down to her sides, frowning curiously as to why.

To see pale hands beneath blood-red robes holding her steady, and sensed the tickle of blonde hair against her cheek.

What?

She gasped.

Oh!

My'ala rose to her feet suddenly, almost teetering over the other way, and turned to catch the whimsical gaze of the God-Elect as he studied her with a smile. Freezing for a moment, the young girl bowed her head and held a hand to her chest, cursing herself inside for being so callous.

What… what's going on?

"No need to fret, my dear," the God-Elect said softly, placing a hand on her shoulder. "You may lift your gaze."

She did so slowly, nauseous and shaking.

"I will say, it was interesting hearing your words – stories about hope, and a path forward from here." His words caught at her ear like lapping waves. "Now I am, in many ways, a light to these people. What I say, cannot escape them, and they will always listen to me." His eyes locked with her own, irises the shade of stardust. "And it seems, then, in an unusual way... that *you* are *my* light in this time of need. For the words you say, seem to shine the brightest..."

Without saying anything more, the God-Elect slipped past the young girl and strode elegantly to the front of the platform, paying no attention to the old woman as she cowered off to one side. As he drew to a halt, he raised his hands to the sky, as if ready to catch the sun.

"Citizens of Arbash!" he boomed commandingly, silencing them at once. "Although it may strike you as unusual, and perhaps even impossible... what the girl says is true. And it comes to no-one as more of a surprise, than it does to me. Because now I see that, if we stay here within these walls, defending against this new threat, we shall only delay what will inevitably come. There is no preserving our way of life, if there is nothing left of it to live. We are, all of us, afraid of what comes next." He clenched his hands into fists. "But we must find hope, in these dark times we face! We must find our true meaning — we must go out into the desert and follow the winds and have faith the God-King will answer us. This haven was built by the hands of the Prophets... now let us, as disciples, forge our own way ahead."

The God-Elect smiled.

"For we are more than just a city: we are a *people*, too!"

What followed, was an eerie silence where not even the crows overhead dared squawk. Ringing out between the streets, echoing up to the walls: a complete and utter lack of sound.

Until the first hands started clapping, followed by several others, and the entire city plaza was awash with applause and cheers were raised all around. My'ala felt her heart sing at the sight of it, her pulse racing as the God-Elect lifted his hand to an almighty bellow from the crowd, cheering his name – cheering for her, the young girl also found, as many hopeful eyes drifted her way too.

Perhaps this is not the end after all, My'ala thought proudly, fires in her eyes.

Perhaps this is simply another beginning…

The God-Elect turned from them after a few moments and paced slowly toward her, the smile welded to his face wickedly.

"Thank you so much, your Elected," My'ala said politely, bowing her head. "Thank you for giving me a chance."

"And thank you, for showing me a better way forward," he replied, bowing his head in return. "You are wise beyond your passage. I'll be keeping a close eye on you for counsel in the future, I reckon…"

He moved past her, gliding across the stonework and back beneath the mobile canopy awaiting him. Adjusting his robes, and without a word more to say, the God-Elect and their entourage moved off toward the palace once more, steeped in shadows and guided by mystery.

How incredible…

My'ala turned back towards the crowd, the heat of the midday sun rebounding off every surface in shimmering rays. The crowd beneath her were already dispersing, returning to their homes to gather their things and prepare for the new way ahead.

The new way ahead, she thought, almost in disbelief.

We did it.

All the fears I had, that this would never work. That people would never listen — that the unknown would scare them too much. Fearing, but at the same time hoping... and now watching that hope blossom before my very eyes. She smiled.

We actually did it...

She turned again, toward the council members off to one side, and found a pair of arms brace her tightly. There were prideful, choking sobs against her neck. My'ala found tears forming at the corners of her own eyes as she returned the embrace, the mellowness of love pulling deep within her.

"I'm so proud of you, Mi," her mother whispered, hands bracing across her back. "I'm so proud of you. I never doubted you..."

"Thank you ma," My'ala replied, resting her head on her shoulder.

"You stood up for yourself, for all of us. You said what you believed in, and people listened. You did what was best for all of us... in your own, wonderful way." Her mother stepped back, and scoffed with joy. "I always knew you were way beyond your rains, Mi... and now look at you, saving our people! You really are remarkable."

She wiped the tears from her cheeks "Well, I learned it from the best: lead with love, and the rest shall follow."

"And I could not be prouder of you, my dear." Her mother paused. "Now we best go and prepare: it turns out we have a lot of packing to do!"

"Yes, ma, of course," My'ala agreed, nodding. "I'll come help with packing…"

But an emptiness swelled in her heart suddenly, opening out like a chasm, and the young girl closed her eyes. A sigh, and a deep sadness, escaped her lips.

"But later, before we depart," she exclaimed, "there's one more thing I have to do…"

XII

THE STARS

As night descended, and the wandering lights of enemy torches scoured the olive grows in the valley, My'ala knew that she had to be quick – or the chance would never come again.

She stayed low to the ground, stooping like a spider, using the bare rows of clementine bushes to hide her movements. She was cautious and light on her feet, moving in fits and starts toward the rise of the hill. There were torches in the grove a few rows down from where she was, the guttural mumblings of the enemy tingling in her ears. She traced the orange aura of their lights as they moved off toward the city, waiting for them to pass her by before chancing a look down toward the sea below.

She found the flickering of fire lights coating the valley

like scabs, with the ugly scars of enemy camps dotted throughout. The painted cove at the base was alive with activity: the shadows of people and supplies and weaponry silhouetted against the moon, intertwining through each other like a colony of ants. That same motion also channelled its way up the cliff-side to her right, as she traced the tiny rivers of people moving back and forth toward the city – and the vast command tents erected just down the hill from Arbash's walls.

They'll be laying siege by the morning, she thought fearfully. *They're already so close... close enough to hear their voices, I imagine. We just have to hope they don't surround the city before sunrise.*

Or else everything we've planned for, is doomed...

The orange light of the nearest patrol swung back toward her suddenly – My'ala dipped back behind the grove, freezing like a gecko as the enemy came and went again, completely unaware of her presence.

Too close. She exhaled through pursed lips.

Now let's find this Hermit, wherever he may be...

She pressed on toward the Sentinel Tree, still stood with its dazzling-white beauty atop the small hill. Under the moonlight, it appeared almost mythical to her: with bark like tiny pebbles, and tiny leaves like emerald gems. My'ala marvelled at it, as she skirted around the far edge of the hill with the expanse of the desert at her back, and scaled up to the base of the tree to hide behind its trunk.

"Artemis!" she whispered, scanning around the roots for his robes. *"Artemis!"*

No response came: there was only the dull whisper of the

wind, and the unsettling grate of moving steel as the patrol drifted off to the south.

"*Artemis!*"

Still no response came.

Where is he? she thought, biting her lip, suddenly very aware of the possibility that he had gone altogether. *Or worse, that he's been taken by the enemy——*

"Hello my dear."

My'ala jumped, holding her hand to her mouth to stifle a scream. She looked to the right, seeking the voice… to find the old red robes and curled grey beard of Artemis, who drew long pulls from a slender wooden pipe held deftly through his fingers.

And as she studied his face, and the stars of his eyes, she also found he was smiling.

"Don't scare me like that, you old fool!" she said, containing her laughter. "I almost gave us away!"

"Should be more vigilant, really," he cooed. "What good is being quiet, if you're blind as a sand-mole?" He grinned, exhaling a wisp of smoke that drifted silently into the night air. "How come you're here, anyway? It's rather dangerous out here, with those patrols about."

"Well, I… I…" My'ala drew still, sensing a pit open in her heart. She sighed. "I'm here because… I'm sorry. I'm sorry for how I acted yesterday. I'm sorry for letting my grief and frustration get the better of me, and that I took it out on you. That wasn't fair, when all you've done is help me… so, I'm sorry, Artemis, for letting you down."

He nodded without a word, glinting stars in his eyes. "You have far from let me down, My'ala, I assure you that. You were, as you said, experiencing a monumental amount of grief about the loss of your brother. You were in a difficult place. And, you let your brother go out there and fight… because you let him pursue his meaning of life, which would not have been a consideration… had it not been for me." It was the Hermit's turn to sigh. "So, in part, I apologise too. Some of your anger was justified toward me, for what happened as a result of those beliefs…"

"I will never blame you for my brother's death, Artemis," she said simply. "I can't… because he died of his own choices, not mine or yours. He died doing what he felt was right, and that's all there is to it." She paused. "And, in that same sentiment, I suppose there is also a thank you to be given."

The Hermit frowned, taking another draw of his pipe. "Whatever for?" he asked.

"Because you were right… about everything. It *is* in the darkest places that the light we seek shines brightest. It's the inevitable joy of hitting rock bottom: because there is no way down from there. And walking back through the city yesterday evening – seeing the sheer grief that consumed everyone I passed – I saw that with my own eyes. How *pained* everyone was… how hopeless and lost we all were. We had consigned ourselves to fate, thinking there was nothing left. But then the next day, before the council could give the verdict, someone spoke up about hope: about the chance we had to forge a new path out into the unknown, for the betterment of everyone. That the idea we could salvage our lives back when the enemy march through our streets… was a falsehood. That we needed a genuine change." She found a small smile. "That we needed another path…"

"And who was that person, who stood up to them and talked of these things?"

My'ala looked up to the moon above, and the vastness of the starlit sky.

"I was."

The Hermit turned to her. "Then I am more proud of you than I can fathom the words for, my dear… truly."

"Thank you," My'ala replied softly, watching the twinkle in his eyes. "It was all you, really, in the end: everything you said to me, led to that point."

"But you were the one that did it. You were the one that took the stand and said it. I played no part in that – *that,* was entirely through you."

"I suppose that's true, yes." She looked to her hands for a moment, thinking deeply, and sensed the tree above her lean over to listen. "I, um… I also had a revelation, while I was up there talking to the crowds," she admitted. "Almost as if the clouds parted and the light shone through."

The Hermit sat forward. "And what was that, my dear?"

She steadied herself. "I think I know what the meaning of life is… and I think you know it too, without even realising it."

Artemis looked intrigued and spun his hand in circles, offering her to continue.

My'ala closed her eyes.

Here we go.

"You have the night sky in your eyes," she began, "because that is where you look to find your answers. You gaze up to the stars, and the moon, hoping one day the truth will come — because in the vast and incomprehensible sky above us, there must be *something* up there for you.

"But I think, deep down… you never really expected to find your answers there. You don't expect a star to fall into the desert, carrying with it the secrets of life. You don't expect to see a message written in a constellation, revealing our true nature. And you never have. Because you know that that reality doesn't exist. That isn't how life works. Because looking up into the night sky and awaiting the answers… well, that's nothing more than a misconception.

"Because you don't seek the answers — you seek the unknown. You accept that the night sky above us is infinitely complex, and yet we know next to nothing about it. We aspire to know more, yet fear how we can get there. Because the unknown is an uncertainty, but it is also our greatest hope.

"So when you look up at the night sky, pondering what's up there, and what meaning we could possibly possess… you have actually been experiencing the meaning of life all along." My'ala smiled. "Curiosity. Fear. Exploration. *The unknown.* Like a young couple, debating having their first child; a farmer, planting their first crop; an angler, casting their first line. Taking a step into the dark — a leap of faith, even. It's what drives us, that terrifying beauty the unknown possesses. It gives us purpose and motivation every single day to do more, learn more, think more. It is as uncertain as the desert sands before us, or the night sky above our heads. But that is also what makes it incredible: with hope, it can be whatever we want it to be. All it takes is a single step, and the world can change forever.

"So when you look up at the sky at night, and seek within you the meaning of life… remember how far you've come, and revel in the beauty of the unknown both past and present. Because it is the unknown that gives us purpose every single day – and all we need to do it, is hope."

The Hermit listened to her intently as she spoke, the shimmering orbits of his eyes spinning with untold beauty. Mesmerised by her revelation – captivated by the truth behind it. Watching as the pieces pulled together, and the oasis emerged from the mirage. And when she had finished explaining, he drew a long pull of his pipe, and blew a stream of smoke into the cool night air.

"To think, it was in my eyes the whole time," he said softly. "The meaning of life, found in the beauty of the unknown… how incredible." He closed his eyes. "Thank you, My'ala, for coming to see me. Despite the risks… thank you for coming here to me, and showing me what you've discovered. Because you are as remarkable as you are gifted, my dear: I don't think I would have ever found the answers had it not been for you. So thank you, for bringing that to me. It has been an honour to have known you all these years, and to have unravelled our true purpose in this world together. In reality, I was little more than a teacher, and you were my student through and through. But now I see things differently… I see, I believe, who you really are."

"How do you mean?"

"Well, I am little more than a wanderer, now satisfied with the answers I have sought for so long." He turned to her then, a radiance in his gaze. "And you, My'ala, are a leader of people, following your purpose into the sun."

Artemis put a hand on her shoulder.

"You... are a *Prophet.*"

My'ala stuttered, her body so light it seemed it would float away. The weight of his hand on her shoulder felt impossible. The sky flushed with light and beauty over the sea. She made to rebuke his words, claiming to be unfit for such a title, but then the Sentinel Tree rustled above her head and its roots seemed to nudge into her affectionately. A sign, perhaps. A truth, maybe.

A prophet? she thought, blinking slowly.

A prophet...

"And now, you must take that mantle on, and do as a Prophet does," Artemis proclaimed.

"What do you mean?" My'ala said shakily.

"You must lead your people to safety, my dear. The caravans will leave soon – the God-Elect is readying the horses as we speak. It's only a matter of time before the evacuation starts. You must be there with your family, at the front of it. That is the only way..."

"What? Wait, how do you know this? How... I don't understand."

"The world is full of secrets my dear – and some, shall never be known." He winked at her, lying back against the tree and closing his eyes.

"But what about you?" My'ala pleaded. "The enemy will find you, if you don't come with us. They'll imprison you. They'll... I can't let that happen..."

"That won't happen, my dear, I promise you."

"Why? How do you know that for sure?"

The Hermit smiled warmly – the smile of a man at peace, like the still waters of a calm sea. "Because my time… has come," he admitted. "My time has come to move on from this world, and let my essence return to the earth and bring renewed life to the land. I have not been well for some time, as you know… and I feel this may be the end of the road."

"Wait, *no!*" My'ala's voice cracked, trembling. "You can't go, you can't… I need you, Artemis! I need you with me, out in the desert. I don't know what to do, I don't…"

"You don't need me, my dear. You don't need me to guide you anymore. You have found your truth, and your path. It is your people and your family who now need you, and you in turn need them. There is no stopping death when it comes… such is the inevitability of life. But what I will say is, you have my thanks, My'ala… for I may now die a happy man, knowing the meaning of life is with me…"

The young girl watched a tear trickle down his cheek like a pearl, and felt her soul weep softly in her chest.

Without saying anything, she wrapped her arms around the Hermit and embraced him tightly, resting her head against his. And for some time, the old wanderer simply sat still, letting her be – until two gnarled hands were placed across her back, and he embraced her in return.

"Thank you for everything, Artemis," she whispered. "I will never forget you."

"Thank you, My'ala, for showing me the truth of this wonderful world that we live in," the Hermit replied. "I am forever in your debt."

They pulled apart, the young girl stepping back and brushing the dust from her legs.

She smiled. "You were an amazing teacher."

Artemis bowed his head. "And you will be a great Prophet, My'ala. Never forget that." He raised his hand. "Now go, my dear… your destiny awaits you."

My'ala nodded, looking off to the south for a moment to follow the orange glow of torches drawing closer to the hill. She inhaled deeply, turning and moving off down the side of the hill, back toward the sheltered groves snaking off to the city in the distance. And as she walked, a few moments passed, until she stopped herself and looked back.

To find, with a tear in her eye, that Artemis the Hermit was gone.

And only hope awaits…

Epilogue

THE CRESCENT MOON

Three days later…

The patrol departed from the southern gate of Arbash in the early passage of morning, with the orange sunlight blanched across their backs and spilling down the valley below. Beyond the scree of vultures on the distant cliffs, and the rustle of leaves in the olive groves at their sides, the soldiers looked around at the eerie silence of the world and scoffed.

"So, they're really gone?" one of them asked, tracing fingers through the fine leaves. "All of them?"

The other soldier pointed off behind them, tracing from the city's east gate out into the desert. "Caravan tracks lead out over the dunes that way, toward the horizon," they replied. "There's no sign of anyone or anything left within the city itself: as far as we know, they simply upped and left with everything they could carry, out into the unknown…"

"The fools." The soldier shook his head. "There's nothing out there but sand and rocks. They'll be taken by the winds soon enough. Nothing survives long out there."

"It's the dishonour, more than anything… imagine not standing up for your city and your homes, when an enemy comes knocking."

"It seems they saw some sense."

"And then threw it all away by heading east…"

"How about that…"

They reached the base of a small hill, gazing up in marvel at the pale tree swaying gently at its peak.

"I've never seen a tree like that before," one of the soldiers remarked. "Have you?"

"Never," said the other. "It looks so old… wonder how long it's been there?"

"Probably as long as the city has. Maybe older still. And apparently it's of some importance to the locals, as they haven't chopped it down for firewood yet."

"Unusual to find trees out here, in a place so barren." The soldier scratched at his beard. "Must be a very special tree."

"Yea… must be."

They reached the top of the hill, and studied around the roots weaving through the earth at their feet. In several places, they noted furrows in the ground where people had sat or moved, and the near-imperceptible marks of footsteps going to and fro.

"People have been up here recently," the bearded soldier said, tracing the impressions in the earth with his finger.

"You can see where they've sat."

"Why would they come all the way out here to sit beneath a tree?" the other inquired, looking up into the sparse boughs above his head.

"Maybe it's a meeting place?"

"Or a place of worship. Perhaps the tree has some link to whatever pagan god they worshiped."

"We saw a lot of prayer-houses in the city, so that might be the case."

The other soldier shook his head. "I do wonder what they hoped to find out here, making their prayers and asking their questions of the world. Did they really expect something to answer?"

"A pointless act, praying to something they can never understand."

"Must be hoping to gain their favour, or something."

"Well, it seems they may need it, the way they're going." The bearded soldier looked out to the desert and laughed. "Hoping their pagan gods can save them from the wrath of the desert… they'll be dead within a week."

"And their bones will be lost to the sands, and we shall rule here unquestioned."

"As all things should be."

The other soldier smiled. "Right you are, my friend."

The bearded soldier gave a snort, looking back for a moment to the vast, abandoned city at their backs. That there, before them, lay the greatest kingdom the desert had ever seen, left empty for them to occupy without a whisper of resistance. The soldier smirked at just how easy it had been: how the people had rolled over like lost dogs and turned tail into the desert, rather than face the enemy that had come to tear their world in two. How foolish they had been; how callously they had thrown their lives away.

How good it felt to rule supreme, so easily.

Turning back to the tree with a coy laugh, eyes flitting across the dry earth at his feet, the bearded soldier stopped suddenly and furrowed his brow.

"You see that?" he asked, pointing to the earth.

The other soldier followed his direction and squinted. "What is that?"

Stooping low, the bearded soldier brushed the layer of sanded dust aside, and pulled at the tiny chain he had found buried beneath.

"What is it?" the other soldier asked.

"It's a.. I don't know what it is."

"What does it mean?"

"I don't know…"

"Who do you think owned it?"

"I'm not sure… but whoever it was, I imagine they had the truth of the world in the palm of their hand, possessing something like this…"

Lifting it to the dawn light, glinting under the jade leaves, the two soldiers gazed at it in wonder.

Studying the silver round, of a crescent moon.

THE END.

ACKNOWLEDGEMENTS

This book is very important to me.
As a long-term sufferer of mental health problems, diagnosed
with Chronic Fatigue Syndrome (CFS), I never thought I would
write a book about the meaning of life – as I have, so often, been
without one.

But this book also came at a time in my life when I needed it
most. While writing these pages, I completely changed my life
around. I took perhaps the biggest leap into the unknown that I
have ever made – and it terrified me. But this book has taught
me (as I hope it may also show you) that life is not about ending
chapters.
It's about starting them.

So, I want to thank my family, my friends, and the indie writing
community as a whole – because without their combined efforts,
I never would have made it to where I am now, doing what I
love every single day.

And, as a final note, this book is dedicated to Bonnie, my old
family dog.
She was a Border Collie, white with black spots, who liked
Frisbees and ham. She was my best friend, and showed me
purpose in life for fifteen long and wonderful years.

So, this one's for you, Bonz.
I miss you everyday.

9 781399 924757